The Secret

Charlotte Brontë

ET REMOTISSIMA PROPE

Hesperus Classics

Hesperus Classics
Published by Hesperus Press Limited
4 Rickett Street, London sw6 1RU
www.hesperuspress.com

First published by Hesperus Press Limited, 2006
'The Secret' and 'Lily Hart' © Hesperus Press, 2006
Foreword © Salley Vickers, 2006

Designed and typeset by Fraser Muggeridge studio
Printed in Jordan by National Press

ISBN: 1-84391-125-6

CONTENTS

FOREWORD

Reading the Brontës' juvenilia leaves one with a slight feeling of literary voyeurism. The stories that the four beleaguered young people, Charlotte, Emily, Anne and Branwell, wrote to and for each other were their private lifelines in the social desert of the Haworth home, which proved the crucible of some exceptional creative activity.

The stories of other realms, written in minute handwriting in tiny, touching home-made books, are classic examples of the uses of the imagination to escape the limitations of the quotidian, which in the Brontës' case was particularly short on other sources of nourishment. The four siblings invented imaginal worlds that they explored and exchanged with each other, Anne and Emily creating Gondal, about which the latter later wrote some of her most haunting poems, and Branwell and Charlotte Angria.

The two principal stories in this collection, 'The Secret' and 'Lily Hart', are based in Angria, a kingdom located in Africa and peopled by a bizarrely eclectic society that includes the Duke of Wellington (who appears in both stories and in 'The Secret' makes a pivotal appearance).

The stories are essentially fairy tales, and the choice of an African location must have been arrived at as the most extreme known geographical opposite to the chill climate and moorland terrain of its Yorkshires creators. Fairy tales are not expressions of social realism and the city of Verdopolis is no more African than Paris or Vienna. Its aristocratic population, including the aforementioned Duke of Wellington, composed of princes, marquises and earls, live in splendid mansions, surrounded by parklands, fountains and forests. They drive their carriages along tree-lined boulevards, where the shops display plentiful jewels – diamonds, sapphires, rubies, emeralds – designed to open the purses of the well-heeled males' leisured spouses.

The costume, too, is equally magnificent: silk capes, fur-lined gowns, diadems like crescent moons, golden shoes. Yet, inevitably, amid all this is to be found the dove-like simplicity of a woman whose natural delicacy and taste infinitely surpass the cruder manifestations of blood and birth.

This, pretty clearly, is the fantasy figure born out of the adolescent Charlotte's own sexual longings. We know her to have been small and plain, and Marion and Lily are the versions of that state but elevated to a condition of romantic desirability. In time, these fairy-tale figures evolved into Jane Eyre, and later Lucy Snowe, whose smallness of stature and demure looks retain something of the prototypes' improbable allure. Jane and Lucy are, of course, also made of sterner, more prosaic stuff. Yet even in the mature portraits we can detect the fantastic sparkle that allow us to perceive them as credible objects of desire.

In 'The Secret' other nascent traits that are to resurface in the later writings are observable. Here is the sounding out of the male voice, which evolved by extension into the pseudonym of Currer Bell, the male persona under which Charlotte published for most of her life. The narrator of 'The Secret' is the brother of Arthur, Marquis of Douro, the baffled husband of the lovely Marion, and indeed, it turns out, also a son to the illustrious Duke. As someone who has written in a male voice myself, I find it especially intriguing that an adolescent girl should have elected to write so early from a contra-sexual position.

Charlotte began writing the Angria stories in 1829, a few years after the traumatic deaths of her elder sisters, Maria and

Elizabeth, who in significant ways had taken the place in her affections of their dead mother. It is apparent that the stories were both an exercise of the innate talent possessed by the whole family and also a form of imaginative therapy to soften the sharp edges of a life that had already borne some severe blows. The socially elevated, financially disembarrassed, picturesque Angrian world is a happy foil to that of its young authors, who, nevertheless, were avid readers, and whose imaginations were fed, among other literary sources, on the *Blackwood Magazine*, a Tory periodical among whose heroes was the Duke of Wellington. Byron was another favourite, and his flamboyant public image unquestionably informs the romantic male figures whom Charlotte both wrote of and whose perspective she daringly chose to write from.

'The Secret' also figures that other character that is to become central to the mature novels, the passionate governess. However, unlike Jane Eyre or Lucy Snowe, the suppressed emotion finds expression in unmediated villainy. Rejected herself by the glamorous Marquis, the aptly named Miss Foxley sets out to destroy the peace of mind of his young and credulous wife by fiendishly resurrecting the spectre of an old betrothal to a childhood sweetheart, a man believed to be long drowned.

Both 'The Secret' and 'Lily Hart' contain elements of the supernatural, which the young Brontës imbibed from the currently fashionable gothic stories featured in the *Blackwood Magazine*. The drowned lover reappears in ghostly, and ghastly, form to assure Marion that her marriage is legitimate and by this means, coupled with the manly resourcefulness of the Marquis, the jealous machinations of the wicked governess are trounced. 'Lily Hart' plays with a similar theme. A natural affinity between social unequals – Lily is pure and lovely but not of appropriate status to her beloved – leads to a period of enforced separation, and at the moment when the engagement is tested, by the attentions of a potential rival, her lover is visited by the voice of Lily, who, as we later learn, has died in the belief that he is lost to her.

All the stories in this volume betray both the immaturity and the incipient talent of the author. The fantasy is childish, predictable and compensatory, and the language, as you would expect of a young girl, often overblown and arch. And yet behind it there beats the unmistakable pulse of something larger, more ambitious in it project and anarchic, and enthralling, in its scope. The psychology is unsophisticated but not unrealistic, and the stories have flashes of gem-like clarity. In their very awkwardness the themes of hidden emotion, loss and suffering become poignant presages of both the life of this author and the greater works that we know were still to come.

– *Salley Vickers, 2006*

The Secret

CHAPTER ONE

A dead silence had reigned in the Home Office of Verdopolis[1] for three hours on the morning of a fine summer's day, interrupted only by such sounds as the scraping of a penknife, the dropping of a ruler, an occasional cough or whisper, and now and then some brief mandate, uttered by the noble First Secretary, in his commanding tones. At length that sublime personage, after completing some score or so of dispatches, addressing a small, slightly built young gentleman who occupied the chief situation among the clerks, said:

'Mr Rhymer, will you be good enough to tell me what o'clock it is?'

'Certainly, my lord!' was the prompt reply as, springing from his seat, the ready underling, instead of consulting his watch like other people, hastened to the window in order to mark the sun's situation. Having made his observations, he answered:

''Tis twelve precisely, my lord.'

'Very well,' said the Marquis. 'You may all give up then, and see that your desks are locked, and that not a scrap of paper is left to litter the office. Mr Rhymer, I shall expect you to take care that my directions are fulfilled.' So saying, he assumed his hat and gloves, and with a stately tread was approaching the vestibule, when a slight bustle and whispering among the clerks arrested his steps.

'What is the matter?' asked he, turning round. 'I hope these are not sounds of contention I hear.'

'No,' said a broad, carroty-locked young man of a most pugnacious aspect, 'but – but – Your Lordship has forgotten that – that –'

'That what?' asked the Marquis, rather impatiently.

'Oh! Merely that this afternoon is a half holiday – and – and –'

'I understand,' replied his superior, smiling, 'you need not task your modesty with further explanation, Flannagan; the truth is, I suppose, you want your usual largesse. I am obliged to you for reminding me – will that do?' he continued, as, opening his pocketbook, he took out a twenty-pound bank bill and laid it on the nearest desk.

'My lord, you are too generous,' Flannagan began; but the Chief Secretary laughingly laid his gloved hand on his lips, and, with a condescending nod to the other clerks, sprang down the steps of the portico and strode hastily away, in order to escape the noisy expression of gratitude which now hailed his liberality.

On the opposite side of the long and wide street to that on which the splendid Home Office stands, rises the no less splendid Colonial Office; and, just as Arthur, Marquis of Douro, left the former structure, Edward Stanley Sydney departed from the latter; they met in the centre of the street.

'Well, Ned,' said my brother,[2] as they shook hands, 'how are you today? I should think this bright sun and sky ought to enliven you if anything can.'

'Why, my dear Douro,' replied Mr Sydney, with a faint smile, 'such lovely and genial weather may, and I have no doubt does, elevate the spirits of the free and healthy; but for me, whose mind and body are a continual prey to all the heaviest cares of public and private life, it signifies little whether sun cheer or rain damp the atmosphere.'

'Fudge,' replied Arthur, his features at the same time assuming that disagreeable expression which my landlord denominates by the term *scorney*. 'Now don't begin to bore me, Ned, with trash of that description, I'm tired of it, quite; pray have you recollected that today is a half holiday in all departments of the Treasury?'

'Yes; and the circumstance has cost me some money; these silly old customs ought to be abolished, in my opinion – they are ruinous.'

'Why, what have you given the poor fellows?'

'Two sovereigns.' An emphatic 'hem' formed Arthur's reply to this communication.

They had now entered Hotel Street and were proceeding in silence past the line of magnificent shops which it contains, when the sound of wheels was heard behind them and a smooth-rolling chariot dashed up and stopped just where they stood. One of the window glasses now fell, a white hand was put out and beckoned them to draw near, while a silvery voice said, 'Mr Sydney, Marquis of Douro, come hither a moment.'

Both the gentlemen obeyed the summons, Arthur with alacrity, Sydney with reluctance.

'What are your commands, fair ladies?' said the former, bowing respectfully to the inmates of the carriage, who were Lady Julia Sydney and Lady Maria Sneaky.

'Our commands are principally for your companion, my lord, not for you,' replied the daughter of Alexander the First. 'Now Mr Sydney,' she continued, smiling on the senator, 'you must promise not to be disobedient.'

'Let me first know what I am required to perform,' was the cautious answer, accompanied by a fearful glance at the shops around.

'Nothing of much consequence, Edward,' said his wife, 'but I hope you'll not refuse to oblige me this once, love. I only want a few guineas to make out the price of a pair of earrings I have just seen in Mr Lapis' shop.'

'Not a bit of it,' answered he. 'Not a farthing will I give you: it is scarce three weeks since you received your quarter's allowance, and if that is done already you may suffer for it.'

With this decisive reply, he instinctively thrust his hands into his breeches' pockets and marched off with a hurried step.

'Stingy little monkey!' exclaimed Lady Julia, sinking back on the carriage seat, while the bright flush of anger and disappointment crimsoned her fair cheek. 'This is the way he always treats me, but I'll make him suffer for it!'

'Do not discompose yourself so much, my dear,' said her companion. 'My purse is at your service, if you will accept it.'

'I am sensible of your goodness, Maria, but of course I shall not take advantage of it: no, no, I can do without the earrings – it is only a fancy, though to be sure, I would rather have them.'

'My pretty cousin,' observed the Marquis, who, till now, had remained a quiet though much amused spectator of the whole scene, 'you are certainly one of the most extravagant young ladies I know: why, what on earth can you possibly want with those trinkets? To my knowledge you have at least a dozen different sorts of ear ornaments.'

'That is true, but then these are quite of another kind; they are so pretty and unique that I could not help wishing for them.'

'Well, since your heart is so much set upon the baubles, I will see whether my purse can compass their price, if you will allow me to accompany you to Mr Lapis'.'

'Oh! thank you, Arthur, you are very kind,' said Lady Julia, and both the ladies quickly made room for him as he sprang in and seated himself between them.

'I think,' said Maria Sneaky, who has a touch of the romp about her, 'I think when I marry I'll have just such a husband as you, my lord Marquis, one who won't deny me a pretty toy when I have a desire to possess it.'

'Will you?' said Arthur. 'I really think the Turks are more sensible people than ourselves.'

In a few minutes they reached the jeweller's shop. Mr Lapis received them with an obsequious bow, and proceeded to display his glittering stores. The pendants which had so fascinated Lady Julia were in the form of two brilliant little hummingbirds, whose jewelled plumage equalled if not surpassed the bright hues of nature. Whilst she was completing her purchase, a customer of a different calibre entered. This was a tall woman attired in a rather faded silk dress, a large bonnet, and a double veil of black lace which, as she lifted it on entering the shop, discovered a countenance which apparently had witnessed the vicissitudes of between thirty and forty summers. Her features might or might not have been handsome in youth, though they certainly exhibited slight traces of beauty now. On the contrary, a sharp nose, thin blue lips and flat eyebrows formed an assemblage of rather repulsive lineaments, even when aided by highly rouged cheeks and profusely frizzed dark locks.

One would have thought that such a person as I have described would have attracted but little attention from a young and gay nobleman like my brother. He, however, fixed his piercing eye upon her the moment she made her appearance. His gaze, nevertheless, did not indicate admiration, but rather curiosity and contempt; a keenly inquisitive expression, mingled with one of scorn, filled his countenance while he watched her.

With a slow and stiff movement she approached the counter, and addressing a shopman, desired to look at some rings. He instantly lifted the glass case and exposed to her view several hundreds of the articles she wanted. Deliberately the lady examined them all, but not one would suit her. Diamonds, rubies, pearls, emeralds, topaz were each in their turn inspected and rejected. At length the shopman, who was

7

a little out of patience at her extreme fastidiousness of choice, enquired what description of ring she could possibly want, since the first jeweller's depot in Verdopolis did not contain it.

'The ring I am in quest of,' replied she, 'should be very small, of plain gold with a crystal stone, containing a little braided chestnut-coloured hair and this name (taking a scrap of paper from her reticule) engraven on the inside.'

'Well, madam,' answered he, 'we certainly have not just such an article as that in the shop at present, but we could very easily make one for you.'

'Could you finish it today?' asked she.

'Yes.'

'Then do so, and I will call for it this evening at nine o'clock.'

With these words she turned to leave the shop. Her eyes, as she lifted them from the counter, fell on the Marquis and met his scrutinising glance. For a moment she seemed to quail under its influence, but presently recovering herself, dropped him a low curtsey, which was returned by a very slight and haughty bow, and sailed into the street.

'Who is that odd-looking woman?' asked Lady Julia as she drew on her gloves, having finally completed her tedious bargain.

The Marquis made no answer; but Maria Sneaky said, with an arch look, 'Some *ci-devant chère amie*[3] of Douro's, I suppose; or perhaps a lady who will hereafter partake with me the benefits of a matrimonial dispensation.'

'Is it so, Arthur?' enquired his cousin.

'Nay, Julia, I shall not tell you. You may draw your own inferences from the circumstances of the case.'

When he had assisted the ladies to their chariot, received his due tribute of parting smiles and thanks, and beheld the brilliant equipage roll merrily off, my brother turned down Hotel Street and directed his steps towards Victoria Square. A thoughtful and somewhat moody cloud darkened his brow as he entered Wellesley House, ascended the grand staircase, and proceeded through a succession of passages and chambers to the Marchioness' apartment. On opening the door, and drawing aside the green damask curtain which hung within, he found her seated alone at a table and engaged in finishing a pencil sketch. She raised her head as he approached and welcomed him with a smile whose sweetness was more eloquent than words.

'Well, Marian,' said he, bending over her to look at the drawing, 'what is this you are about?'

'Only a little landscape, my lord, which I sketched in the valley yesterday.'

'It is really very pretty, and most charmingly pencilled; I think I remember the view. Is it not from the gateway of York Villa?'

'Yes, Arthur, and I have introduced Mr Sydney in the foreground with a book in his hand.'

The Marquis now sat down beside his wife and continued for some time silently watching the progress of her pencil. At length he recommenced the conversation by saying, 'Whom do you think I have seen in the city today, Marian?'

'I'm sure I don't know; perhaps Julius. I desired Mina to take him out for an airing about half an hour since.'

'No, you are far wrong in your guess.'

'Who, then?'

'No other than your old governess, Miss Foxley.'

At hearing this name, the colour faded from Marian's cheek. She paused in the midst of her employment, and slowly raising her large blue eyes from the paper, fixed them on

Arthur with a look of deep alarm. He observed her agitation, and the thoughtful aspect of his countenance darkened into something like displeasure as he continued:

'What, Marian, is not that inexplicable spell yet broken? I thought absence and kind treatment might do much, but it appears all my affection has not yet succeeded in erasing that impression which, by some mysterious means, Miss Foxley contrived to make on your too sensitive mind.'

Tears now began to fill the Marchioness' eyes and were dropping unheeded on her drawing as she answered, in a subdued tone, 'Do not be angry, Arthur.'

'I am not angry, Marian,' he replied, 'but can you deny that it was owing to that creature's cursed influence that you so long and steadfastly refused my hand, heart and coronet – even when, as you have so often confessed, your inclination was not averse to the offer and when, as I could perceive, a final rejection would have blasted your happiness for life? Is it not from that cause that those transient periods of melancholy arise, with which you are even now oppressed?' Marian made no answer; he went on. 'How you at length summoned sufficient courage to throw off her shackles and consent to felicity I know not, nor is my penetration sufficiently keen to divine; but it appears there are yet some lingering remains of her power. Come, Marian, dismiss this weakness. How can she hurt you whilst under my protection? Make me your father confessor – you cannot find one more indulgent – and reveal all.'

Still there was no reply. The Marquis now rose in anger. 'This is obstinacy, Marian,' he said, 'as well as weakness. I shall leave you for the present to reflect on the consequences of a continuance in such folly, but first let me warn you that I shall not suffer that woman to enter my house, or permit you to have any communication with her; and if I find my commands in this respect are disobeyed, I shall consider our interests as thenceforth separate. It is no part of my plan to allow the existence of a counteracting influence to my own in that heart and family where I ought to reign paramount.'

With these words he closed the door, and in a few minutes the echo of his receding footsteps died away along the distant corridor.

It may perhaps be necessary to give my reader a more particular account of Miss Foxley before I proceed with my narrative. This I shall do in as few words as possible. She was the only child of a respectable merchant who died insolvent, leaving her an orphan, at the age of twenty-one, with no other fortune than her accomplishments – which were numerous – and her abilities – which, though not of the highest order, were nevertheless of a kind well fitted to enable her to push her way through the world, consisting chiefly in a capacity of discovering people's natural dispositions and adapting herself to them so as to worm a way into their good graces, and a certain sharp-sighted shrewdness wherever her own interests were concerned. In early youth she was not devoid of personal graces; but her beauty bore no proportion to her vanity, and any wound in that quarter never healed, but continued to fester till revenge in some tangible shape was achieved on the offending person. On her father's death, being unable to support herself in independence, she entered the family of the late Lady Hume in the situation of companion, and, as such, contrived so far to secure the confidence of that amiable and unsuspicious woman that on the birth of Marian she was appointed governess, for which office she was well qualified as far as talents and acquirements went. After Lady Hume's death, which took place when her daughter was fourteen years old, Miss Foxley still continued to reside at Sir Alexander's residence in Wellington's Land and was there when Arthur began to pay his addresses to her lovely young pupil. Unfortunately, the governess, who had now numbered her thirty-fifth year, was prompted by her inextinguishable vanity to imagine that she yet possessed charms potent enough to attract the admiration of a handsome and high-born nobleman. Under the influence of this delusion, she employed every art to draw away my brother's affections from the little unsophisticated girl who, in her opinion, knew not how to appreciate their value. Her efforts, however, were unsuccessful; they excited disgust instead of love, and at length, one afternoon when she was even more than usually forward, Arthur plainly though politely intimated that she was rather too old and obscure to form a fit wife for him. This was sufficient to kindle all the bad passions in Miss Foxley's mind. She vowed mentally to make him regret his cold and scornful rejection, and thenceforth set herself sedulously to work in order to prevent his union with her beautiful and youthful rival.

The effect of her endeavours soon became but too apparent. For some time Marian carefully avoided her noble lover, refused his hand, shunned his attentions, and so managed that Arthur, Marquis of Douro, the proudest and haughtiest youth of Verdopolis, was reduced to the condition of a pining, consumptive, lovesick young gentleman. Meantime, it was universally believed in the city that the delay of his union with the daughter of Sir A. Hume was owing to my father's opposition. How great would have been the surprise of all ranks had it been known by whom the objection was really started. It was evident, however, that Miss Hume's perseverance in this course was not unattended with pain to herself: her wan looks, attenuated form and tearful eyes soon proclaimed that there was a wasting worm within. Still, however, she constantly refused to listen to my brother's passionate professions; and the triumph of Miss Foxley's intrigues was nearly completed when one day Arthur, having resolved to make a last attempt and then give up in despair, arrived at Badey Hall; to his astonishment he was at once shown into Marian's drawing-room, where he found her alone. What eloquent arguments he made use of to plead his cause, I know not; certain it is, however, that he was this time successful, and three weeks after, his lovely tyrant, amidst smiles, tears and blushes, pledged her troth to him at the high altar of St Michael's Cathedral. The first act of his authority as a husband was to command the immediate dismissal of Miss Foxley, who was consequently turned to the right about. He subsequently attempted to win from Marian an explanation of the causes which had so long delayed his happiness, but on this subject she maintained a mysterious silence, and he had for some time ceased to trouble her about it, till the governess' reappearance brought it again most unpleasantly to his memory.

When the Marquis was gone, Marian, with a deep sigh, bent again over her half-finished picture, but now the pencil seemed to have lost its power, or the hand which directed it its skill. Instead of the flowing, correct lines and soft shadows which she had before produced, tremulous, wavering strokes and dark blotches mocked her unavailing efforts. At last she relinquished the attempt, and after replacing the sketch in her portfolio and closing the ivory box which contained her drawing materials, she drew towards her a harp which stood near. At first her slender, snowy fingers only extracted a few melancholy though sweet notes from the quivering strings; but soon these unconnected sounds gave place to a melody simple yet exquisitely plaintive; and ere long the according tones of her flutelike voice changed it to a delicious harmony while she sang the following little metrical fragment:

On the shore of the dark, wild sea,
Alone I am roaming,
While sounds its voice mournfully
Through the deep gloaming.

Oh! those deep, hollow tones
Sad thoughts inspire,
They swell like the thrilling moans
From breeze-swept lyre.

Echoes from rock and cave,
Solemnly dying,
Answer the howling wave,
Mock the wind's sighing.

Far in the silent sky,
Wandering worlds quiver;
Thus they shall beam on high,
Changeless for ever.

But ere another moon
Silvers the billow,
Ocean will be my tomb,
Sea-sand my pillow.

Then my unhallowed name
None shall remember:
Gone like the dying flame,
Quenched like the ember.

There were yet two verses of the fragment unsung, when she was interrupted by a rap at the door.

'Come in,' said the Marchioness, and Mina entered, carrying a lovely infant.

'Well, my darling,' exclaimed she, as with an assumed expression of cheerfulness she rose and held out her arms to receive the pretty scion. 'How are you after your walk?'

'The fresh air has brought a little colour into his cheeks, my lady,' replied Mina, relinquishing her charge.

'I see it has, and since that is the case, you had better take him out daily for the future, Mina.'

'Yes, I shall, my lady,' replied the waiting-maid, seating herself at a small work table and taking up a white robe which she had previously been embroidering for her mistress.

Marian for a few minutes continued talking to her little Julius and endeavouring to amuse him with the coral and gold bell suspended round his waist; but soon sad thoughts seemed to come over her mind, for she ceased to speak and sat gazing on the child with eyes of mournful meaning. Mina, who is a shrewd, penetrating girl, firmly attached to the Marchioness and high in her confidence, presently perceived this depression of spirits, and desirous to learn the cause of it, she broke silence by saying, 'I fear something has happened to vex my lord.'

'What makes you think so?' asked Marian, starting.

'Because when I met him on the strand a little while since, he neither spoke to me nor Lord Julius, as he always does if he is in a good temper, but passed on with a grave, sorrowful look, though the little darling cried to go to him.'

To these words the Marchioness made no reply, and Mina, resuming her work, continued to trace the rich pattern in silence. They continued thus employed for about half an hour, when a second rap was heard at the door. Mina rose to open it; a footman stood without with a letter.

'Who brought this, William?' asked his lady, after a hasty glance at the seal and direction.

'A little boy, my lady, who said that it had been given him by a woman in Harley Street.'

'Is he gone?'

'Yes, ma'am.'

'Very well, William, that will do.'

Hurriedly Marian broke the seal and ran over the contents of the letter. Her features whitened while she read. At the conclusion it dropped from her nerveless hand, and she would have fallen to the ground, had not the ready Mina been in an instant at her side. Happily she did not faint. On the contrary, a few minutes restored the vanishing rose to her cheek and lip. She then desired to be left alone. 'You may carry your work, Mina, into my dressing room,' said she, 'and take Julius to his nurse. Let no one come here till I ring the bell. I wish to be undisturbed for a short time.'

Mina accordingly withdrew, and it was midnight before she was again summoned to attend her lady. All the other servants had retired to rest an hour before, and she alone remained in the deserted hall, anxiously awaiting the expected sound. At length, just as she had formed the resolution to go un-called, twelve o'clock struck and the wished-for tinkle sounded.

On opening the sitting-room door, she saw the Marchioness placed exactly as she had left her, in a chair near the hearth, resting her head against the mantelpiece. There was no candle in the apartment, and in the grate the last feeble embers were just expiring.

'Will you not go upstairs now, my lady?' asked Mina. 'I have brought your bedroom lamp.'

'No, Mina, not yet. But come in, I want to speak to you.'

The waiting-maid closed the door and sat down in a chair which her mistress pointed out. Marian then continued, 'You know the Marquis, Mina, as well as I do, and that being almost perfect himself, he cannot brook imperfection in others. His word and command have hitherto been my law, to which I have always submitted myself with cheerfulness and pleasure. Tonight, however, I am going to set in direct opposition to his will. Utter necessity must plead my excuse for such otherwise unpardonable disobedience; but if he discovers it, I am lost. Do you know where Harley Street is, Mina? I must go there this night.'

'No, my lady, I do not; but surely you do not intend to go alone?'

'Yes, I do.'

17

'That cannot be, my lady. You would be lost in the city. Do let my father go with you; he knows every street and lane of Verdopolis.'

Is he in the house?'

'Yes, my lord ordered him to sleep here every night.'

'Call him, then.'

Mina left the room and in about ten minutes returned accompanied by her father. Ned halted at the door for a moment. 'Come in, Edward,' said the Marchioness in her sweet, mild tone.

'I was only stripping my shoes, my lady,' said he, ''cause they're not fit to walk on such a grand carpet as this.'

'Oh, never mind that,' replied she with a faint smile at his punctilious decorum. 'I am sorry to have called you from your bed, Edward, but I wished to learn from you what quarter of the city Harley Street is situated in.'

'Harley Street? Why, it's the same as they call Paradise Street, my lady, 'cause there's a house in it that you wouldn't like to pass by yourself at this time of night.'

'Should I not? Then will you go with me?'

'That I will, with all the pleasure in life.'

'Fetch my hat and cloak, then, Mina.'

'Had you not better take mine, my lady?' asked the prudent *fille de chambre*.

'Yes, on second thoughts that would certainly be the best.'

Mina again left the room and shortly came back with a plain straw hat and brown silk mantle. In these she attired her young mistress, and then, after lighting the fair adventurer and her guide down a private staircase to a street door, of which she possessed the key, returned to the servants' hall, and stretching herself on a chintz sofa that stood at the side of the still blazing hearth, was soon buried in a profound sleep.

The night was wild and stormy; vast, billowy clouds, from which a drizzling rain incessantly distilled, rolled over the sky, and at times, as they parted their folds, the serene moon was revealed shining far beyond them. A chill north wind mingled its moaning with that of the troubled sea, whose howling waves might now be heard uttering their voice afar off. With a light step and beating heart, Marian trod the wet, gloomy streets, preceded by her trusty conductor. After passing through many wide squares and long, broad streets, they entered a dark lane which would scarcely admit more than four persons abreast. On one side a line of lofty buildings arose, in the centre of which a sudden burst of moonlight discovered a flight of steps surmounted by a portico.

'This is Harley Street, my lady,' said Ned, stopping and turning around.

'Is it, Edward?' replied she in a low tone; and then, as if seized with a sudden agitation, she sank on the steps before mentioned.

Scarcely had she sat there for five minutes, when the sound of many footsteps was heard approaching. All was now again dark, so that nothing could be distinguished; but as the persons drew near, Marian easily recognised several by their voices.

'I think, Vice-President, we are late tonight,' said one in a deep, calm tone.

'Yes, most worthy[4],' was the reply, uttered in a voice which struck chill dismay to the Marchioness' heart and caused her instantly to take refuge behind a sort of projecting pillar. 'Yes, we are, and I'll wager ten to one that Gordon proposes to fine us for it.'

'Taken, my lord Marquis,' exclaimed another.

'Is that O'Connor?' asked the former speaker.

'Yes.'

'Done, then, and I hope to fleece you well, my most excellent knight of the mattock.'

Here the door within the vestibule opened and a sudden glare of lamps streamed on the dense, dark night, revealing the forms of about twenty or thirty gentlemen, most of them tall handsome men.

Pride in their port, defiance in their eye,
These mighty lords of humankind passed by.[5]

Tumultuously they sprang or rushed up the steps into a vast and magnificent hall, blazing with sun-like chandeliers which appeared above. Then the door closed and Night reassumed her solemn, silent reign.

'Those are rare chaps,' said Ned, as he rejoined the terrified Marchioness. 'If they had seen you, there would have been some'at to do; only His Lordship was there, and that would have checked them a bit, I guess.'

'Let us proceed now, Edward,' said she.

'Which house are we to stop at, my lady?'

'The last in the street, on the left hand.'

They soon reached it, and Marian, after directing Ned to wait on the outside till she should return, knocked timidly at the door. It was presently opened by a dirty-looking servant wench in a dingy lace cap and gaudy cotton gown.

'Is there not a lady of the name of Miss Foxley lodging here?' asked the Marchioness.

'Yes, madam, and if you'll follow me I'll show you her apartment.' Accordingly, after carefully fastening the door, she led the way up a narrow flight of stone steps and through a sort of lobby, which was dimly lighted by a single lamp, to a room at the further end. Entering first, she announced that the lady was come.

'Indeed,' said someone within; 'bring her here directly'; and the visitor was ushered into a small chamber, whose furniture consisted of a mahogany pembroke table, five or six cane-bottomed chairs, a scanty carpet, faded green window curtains, and a broken paper screen. A small but bright fire burnt in the grate, and beside it a tall female was seated in an armchair. She rose as Marian entered and advanced to meet her, saying, 'My lady Marchioness, how are you? I am surprised at your condescension in deigning to visit so obscure an individual as myself. Pray be seated, if these poor chairs are not too mean to support a peeress of the realm.'

'Miss Foxley,' replied the Marchioness, as she took the offered seat, 'I have run considerable risk in complying with your request; nor am I sure that my conduct in this respect is right; but my anxiety to learn the truth of what your letter hinted at induced me to disregard all other considerations. Pray give me a more explicit account without delay.'

'Why, madam!' returned the governess, with a fiendlike smile. 'You are doubtless now a happy wife, loving and beloved. The Marquis, by all accounts, makes a fond husband; and a son, I understand, has lately crowned your felicity. But, my lady, is not this bliss too perfect to endure? Do you not dread an interruption? A profound calm is gener-ally succeeded by a storm. Do you not know of one whose appearance would utterly blast all this course of ecstatic pleasure?'

'Miss Foxley, Miss Foxley,' murmured Marian, in a scarcely audible tone, 'don't torture me so, for Heaven's, for my mother's sake, whom you once respected. End this suspense and let me know the worst. Is he returned?'

'I will show you,' answered Miss Foxley, ringing the bell, which was almost instantly answered by the servant-maid. 'Tell the gentleman in the next room I wish to speak with him,' said she.

The girl departed, and almost immediately after a young man entered the room. He was tall and genteelly formed, with brown hair, wild dark eyes and a handsome though meagre countenance.

'Mr Henry,' said Miss Foxley, 'allow me to introduce your early friend, Marian Hume, to you. Now, unfortunately, she bears another surname, but that is not my fault.'

He approached the Marchioness, who sat with her face buried in her hands, and said, 'Madam, permit me to announce myself as that long-absent Henry Percy, who once, at least, was honoured with your regard.'

At the sound of his voice, she raised her head, looked at him fixedly for some minutes, and then replied, 'This is not, cannot be Henry. He was younger, fairer, his voice softer. Miss Foxley, you are deceiving me; this person scarcely resembles him in the least.'

'That may be,' answered the governess, 'yet, notwithstanding, he is Henry Percy, your Henry Percy, and no other.'

'I deny it; here is his picture,' (taking a portrait from her bosom). 'Compare them and tell me where the similitude lies.'

'Madam,' interposed the young man, 'I do not wonder at your denial of my identity. The lapse of time and a long sojourn in foreign climates must necessarily have produced a vast change; but though I may be altered externally, yet within all is as it ever was, which is, I fear, more than can be said of some others.'

'Do not insult me, sir,' said Marian, the deadly white to which her cheek had faded giving place to a bright flush of anger. 'I shall believe the evidence of my senses, rather than your assertions.'

'Since you will not credit my word,' replied he, 'look at this token, and reject its testimony if you dare.'

So saying, he put into her hand a small silver box. She opened it; a single glance at its contents seemed to bring sudden and forcible conviction, for with a faint shriek she sank back in the chair, almost deprived of animation.

'Now, perjured one, do you acknowledge me?' asked Mr Percy with bitter emphasis.

'I do, I do, but oh! spare me for one week: give me at least that time for thought, for consideration.'

'Not a day, not an hour will I spare you! My claim is legal and I will enforce it now.'

The Marchioness then fell on her knees, and with streaming eyes and clasped hands implored a reprieve, however short. Her extreme agony seemed at length to move him.

'Rise, madam,' said he. 'You shall have a week's delay, on condition that you promise not to consult with the Marquis of Douro during that time.'

'And,' added Miss Foxley, 'on condition that you likewise promise to return here tomorrow night in order to receive important information respecting yourself, my lady, which you do not at present appear to be in a situation to listen to.'

'I will promise anything!' exclaimed she, grateful for this temporary relief. 'But of what nature is the information you allude to, Miss Foxley?'

'I merely wish to let you know who and what you are, a circumstance of which you have hitherto been ignorant.'

'Cannot I hear it now?'

'No, it is too late, and the dawn is already rising.'

Marian, then, after some further conversation, took her leave. She found Ned anxiously awaiting her return in the street by the dim light of the breaking day. They hastily trod the path to Wellesley House, where, fortunately, they arrived unobserved. Ned, then, after receiving his young lady's cordial thanks, which he valued even more than the solid reward which accompanied them, retired to enjoy in peace the refreshment of undisturbed slumber. The Marchioness likewise sought her pillow, but sorrow and sad thought banished sleep far from the stately couch where she lay.

On the night after that spoken of in my last chapter, the drawing-room at Ellrington House exhibited a more tranquil scene than it usually does. Instead of the dark political devoir, turbulent and boisterous wine party, or dazzling and bewildering crowd of Fashion's bright devotés, two persons alone, the lord and lady of the mansion, sat one on each side of the cheerful and tranquil hearth. A few wax tapers on the mantelpiece, shining amongst a hundred sparkling decorations aided by the blaze of a clear fire, furnished light sufficient to enable Lord Ellrington to peruse a treatise on the present state of society, and his wife to decipher the characters of a Persian poem. At length the former, after several muttered expressions of contempt for his author, threw down the work and said, 'Come, Zenobia, give up poring over that absurd passion you are at there. I dare say, if one could read it, it's the rarest trash in nature.'

'Indeed, Ellrington, you are mistaken; finer sentiments were never embodied in language. But what book have you been reading all this time?'

'A translation into the English tongue of an ass's bray.'

'Indeed? Then you were less profitably employed than my-self. I was construing the song of a nightingale to his favourite rose.'

'And pray, what is the name of the idiot who has conceived that surpassingly magnificent idea?'

'Ferdoona, one of the greatest poets Persia ever produced.'

'And do you really, Zenobia, admire such grovelling nonsense?'

'Most undoubtedly I do.'

'Well, women are the most incomprehensible creatures on earth; sometimes you seem to be possessed of considerable sense and discernment, and then again you commit acts and utter speeches which argue great weakness, if not a total deprivation, of intellect.'

'Granting it is so, Alexander, might I not say the same of you? How often during the revolution of a year are you as rational as at present?'

'If I were not in a particularly easy humour tonight that sentence would stick in my throat, Zenny.'

'Would it? And most likely, in that case, a bottle of wine would be necessary to wash it down.'

'Probably, but tell me, now I think on it, what makes you hide all your hair under that singularly formed cap which you have lately worn?'

'Fashion, my lord, and the caprice of custom.'

'What? Does fashion induce the ladies to destroy their beauty?'

'Sometimes, but since you dislike it, the defect is easily remedied.' So saying, she plucked out the comb which confined her hair, and immediately a cloud of raven tresses fell down in rich profusion over her neck and shoulders.

'There,' said Ellrington after a moment's silence, 'you look like yourself, now. It is astonishing what a difference the presence or absence of a few curled locks makes.'

Pleased with her attention to his wishes, he found himself in a better and more amicable humour than any which had soothed his stormy soul for many a long year, when, just as he had reached the acme of suavity, a rap was heard at the door.

'Come in,' said he, and the servant who stood without was startled at the gentleness of tone in which these words were pronounced, as generally, when he ventured to disturb his master thus, a volley of oaths and curses formed the reward of his pains. Timidly opening the door, he announced that a person wished to speak with Lord Ellrington.

'A person! And pray, what kind of a one is it, coming here at this time of night?'

'It is a woman, my lord, and, I believe, a young one, though she keeps her face so covered with a handkerchief that I can't see it distinctly.'

'Hey! some mystery! Well, show her into the library and say I'll come directly.'

'What can the creature possibly want?' said Lady Zenobia. 'I think, Ellrington, it was foolish of you not to send a denial.'

'Oh! nonsense, Zenny. She may have something particular to tell me, you know.'

When Lord Ellrington entered the library, he perceived a slender female figure attired in a silk mantle and a large straw hat which had fallen back and discovered a luxuriant flow of beautiful chestnut ringlets. Her face was turned away and partially hidden with the palms of her small white hands.

'Well, my girl,' said he, 'what is your business with me?'

At first, she made no answer. He repeated the question. She then slowly lifted her head and discovered a countenance which, bright with blushes and formed in the most exquisite mould of youthful loveliness, appeared an object so fair and fascinating that the lofty nobleman could not restrain an exclamation of surprise. After gazing at her a moment with an astonished air, he said, 'Do I deceive myself, or is this the peerless Marchioness of Douro?'

My lord, your conjecture is right,' replied she, at once seeming to throw off the bashfulness which had before oppressed her and fearlessly meeting his fixed gaze with an eye that sparkled almost with the light of insanity. 'I am that unhappy woman.'

'And to what am I indebted for this unexpected, though most welcome, pleasure?'

'To desperation, my lord. Nothing short of that should have made me humble myself so.'

'I am sorry for that, fair lady, as I hoped you were come of free will; but tell me, in what I can serve you? It shall not be said that the prettiest woman in Verdopolis asked my assistance in vain.'

'Do not talk so, Lord Ellrington,' exclaimed Marian, while a sudden shudder ran through her whole frame. 'Knowing what I know, such light language sounds horrible.'

'And what do you know, my lady?'

'What I would not tell you for worlds and what I am come here in order to confirm, though I fear it scarce needs confirmation.'

'This is mysterious language, I do not understand it.'

'But you will ere long. Tell me, my lord, have you not a casket belonging to the late Lady Percy, which up to this day you have never been able to open?'

'I have, but how in the name of the heavens, the earth, the seas, and all that are therein did you obtain knowledge of it?'

'That I cannot explain to you at present, my lord. Permit me only to see the box, and I will show you a method of opening it.'

'Well, I really cannot refuse a request from such lips, so permit me, my lady Marchioness, to conduct you into the apartment where the object of your curiosity is kept.' With these words, he offered to take her hand. She, however, withdrew it with an apparently involuntary movement of repulsion.

'What?' said he, scowling furiously, 'do you dare to reject in disdain that courtesy which it was almost a condescension for me to offer?'

'I was wrong,' replied Marian, bursting into tears. 'You may take my hand, Lord Ellrington, for I fear you have a right to command me in everything.'

The last words were uttered in so low a tone as to be inaudible to His Lordship. Her tears, however, softened him, as he imagined them to arise from a dread of his anger. He therefore accepted the hand which otherwise might perhaps now have been declined, and taking up a candle, led her out of the room.

They passed in silence across the entrance hall, ascended the grand staircase, and trod with noiseless step the matted floor of a long gallery, at the termination of which was a door. This Lord Ellrington unlocked, and they entered a small apartment panelled with black oak. In the centre of it stood a table covered with papers and in one corner an elaborately carved cabinet in which lay four swords, three sheathed and one naked. Above them hung a large banner, blood-red and bearing for its device a skull and cross-bones in black.

'This,' said the nobleman, after having again locked the door, 'is my *sanctum sanctorum*,[6] lady Marchioness.' He paused and looked steadily upon her, as if to see what impression the scene produced.

It was indeed a strangely awful situation for poor Marian to be placed in. There she stood at the dead hour of the night, alone and face to face with that dark, stern man whose mighty talents and still mightier crimes will hereafter appal the muse of history as she records them. A deep and boding silence reigned around, interrupted only by the faint, dull sound of a closing door or hurried tread from some distant part of the vast mansion, sounds that only served to intimate that help, if needed, was too far off to be obtained. Cold ran the blood to that youthful lady's heart as she thought on these things, but terror so restrained her tongue and fettered her limbs while under the influence of that searching falcon eye, that she neither breathed a word nor moved a finger.

'How do you like it?' he continued with a sardonic smile, lifting the lamp and drawing up his lofty form to all its majestic height. 'You see those four swords and that red flag on the cabinet yonder?'

She bowed.

'Well, now, my lady, I'll tell you what they mean. This is the blade I wielded in my youth, when I killed Negroes for Wellington. This is the weapon that helped me in exile; it is drunk with the blood of merchants by sea and land. And this not many years since, made Alexander the First[7] tremble on his mountain throne. Those three are all sheathed; they have done their work, they have slain their thousands and tens of thousands and now they may rest. But for this other! Look at it, my lady, look at it well. See how sharp and bright and glittering it is – not a spot of blood, not a streak of rust blackens it. This is a virgin sword, it has pierced no heart, freed no spirit; but it lies bare and ready; it bides its time. A voice and a power is in that weapon: the voice shall speak the doom of nations; the power shall execute it. And by the strength of what arm shall it do these things?' he continued, suddenly laying his hand on her shoulder with a force that made her tremble. 'And for what prize will the great game be played? Mine is the arm, a crown is the prize!'

He paused a moment, and then went on again in a lower tone. 'As for that flag, it is the pennon of the Black Rover. For seven years it swept the seas, the dreaded, the invincible. In storm and sunshine, war and mirth, the battle and the festival, she remained unhurt, unchanged. When the waves were strewed with the tempest-torn fragments of the merchantman and the man-of-war, my good ship, their dread and scourge, spread her white sail and, like a haunting spirit of the deep, proudly breasted those waters that none else dared look upon. Men said she was charmed against wind and wave, and they spoke truth, for I trod her deck and directed her course, therefore Destiny with her triple shield ever hovered round –

'But stop! Am I a madman or an idiot, to talk thus to you? Humph! I fear I have been letting out. But it is easy to prevent consequences. Kneel down, Marchioness of Douro, kneel this instant. Dare you resist? There, that is right. You must excuse the push I gave you, but it is always best to obey me at once without hesitation. Now swear by the head of that old man whom you worship never to whisper in mortal ear one word of what I have been saying this night. Swear, or – '

'I do swear,' said she in a faint voice.

'That is well. Get up. You are an obedient and praiseworthy girl, and if I had the management of you would soon arrive at the perfection of feminine meekness of humility.'

Marian rose and stood before the imperious nobleman. She was deadly pale and might have passed for a beautiful marble statue, had not the tremor which shook every limb indicated that her form was of living flesh and blood. Lord Ellrington again fixed his eye on her and seemed to take pleasure in witnessing the profound awe which his keen gaze inspired. At last, after torturing her thus for some minutes, he broke out into a long and loud burst of laughter. She stepped back and looked at him doubtingly, as if she thought his brain disturbed.

'Well,' he exclaimed as soon as the exhaustion arising from his strange fit of merriment would permit him to speak, 'have I frightened you, my lady? Come! nonsense! cheer up! One would think you were never spoken to harshly or looked at sternly before. Pray, does the Marquis never discipline you a little in this way? Confess the truth now, is he not sometimes rather crusty and overbearing?'

'My lord,' stated Marian, while an indulgent blush crimsoned her snowy brow and faded cheek, 'I will not hear my husband's name mentioned thus, even by you, satanically proud as you are –' She would have said more, but the half-formed words died away on her lips, and with them the transient flash of spirit likewise vanished.

'Satanically proud,' muttered Lord Ellrington after her. 'That is daring. You forget, I think, my lady, where you are and how situated; but methinks you need not pretend to be so thin-skinned as it regards the Marquis at the moment when you are committing what in his eyes would unquestionably appear a most deadly offence; for I do not think he is acquainted with this midnight visit to Ellrington House.'

Marian made no reply to this cutting remark; she only sighed deeply. A pause now ensued, during which Lord Ellrington slowly paced the room. It was some time before she ventured to interrupt him by again referring to the business which had occasioned her visit. At length, summoning resolution, she said hesitatingly, 'Can Your Lordship permit me to look at the casket now?'

Without answering, he strode directly to the cabinet and, taking a key from his pocket, unlocked it. A multitude of miscellaneous articles were contained in the different divisions; but in one, more carefully arranged than the rest, there appeared an ivory box inlaid with silver, a long braided lock of beautiful light-brown hair, a lady's watch, and a miniature portrait of a beautiful woman set in a massive gold frame, richly decorated with jewels. He took the box and put it into her hand.

She moved a few paces from him towards the table on which the lamp was placed, and having opened the casket by means of a secret spring, took from it a paper that formed the whole of its contents. This she glanced hastily over, and then, suddenly and before Lord Ellrington could prevent her, consumed it in the flame of the lamp, exclaiming when she had done, 'Thank God that evidence is destroyed.'

'How dare you?' said he, approaching her with angry strides and laying his hand, as if by instinct, on a pistol which appeared half-hidden in his breast. 'If you were a man I'd blow you to atoms for that action this moment.'

'Do it now,' said Marian, perfectly undaunted by his manner, 'and rid me of a life which I have lost the power of enjoying.'

'No,' he replied, thrusting back the pistol, 'I'll not kill you, but I'll do what perhaps in your present state of mind would be almost as bad. I'll keep you locked up here till you tell me, and that truly, the contents of the paper which you have just destroyed.'

'That I will never do; every fresh view which I obtain of your conduct determines me more against it.'

'Is the silly girl mad?' said Lord Ellrington with a gloomy frown. 'Has she forgotten who and what I am?'

'No, my lord, I have not, but the sentiments which I cannot help entertaining against you will force their way despite of all my efforts to restrain them.'

'Note, then, you may take the consequences of your want of self-government, and continue here with me at least till the morning light. If you behave well during the next five or six hours, I may perhaps permit you to return home in time to explain your absence to the Marquis as you best can.'

In vain did Marian endeavour by entreaties, remonstrances and even tears, to turn him from his purpose. He was inexorable; and during the remainder of that night, she was compelled to continue an unwilling prisoner, listening to the keen taunts, false insinuations and detested gallantry of her stern jailer. At last, just as the lamp was beginning to wane before the first pale beams of dawn which shone faintly through the single lofty and narrow window with which the apartment was lighted, a hesitating knock was heard at the door.

'Who's there?' thundered Lord Ellrington.

'It is only I,' replied the voice of his wife, in very subdued tones. 'I wished to know, Alexander, whether you intended to retire to rest at all before morning or not.'

'And how dare you wish to know anything about the matter? Off to your bed this instant, without reply!' Zenobia understood the accent in which her husband spoke and withdrew immediately.

'Now,' said he, turning to the Marchioness, 'I will allow Your little Ladyship to depart. Come along.'

Gladly she followed him as, after unlocking the door, he led the way through gallery, hall and passage to the grand entrance. This he unfastened with his own hands. Marian did not wait for any farewell ceremonies, but darting past him, cleared the steps at a spring, fled down the street with the speed and lightness of a roe, and was out of sight in a twinkling. An effusion of golden light filled the east before she reached Wellesley House. All, however, was still silent around that lordly mansion, and when she rang the bell at the private door it was opened by Mina.

'Oh, my lady,' exclaimed that faithful handmaiden, 'I am so glad you are come. I have passed such a night of suspense and misery on your account as no one ever did before, scarcely.'

'Did the Marquis return home last night?' asked her mistress.

'Yes, he did at four o'clock. I then thought that your absence could not miss being discovered and gave up all for lost; but most fortunately he went to his own bedroom, and therefore everything is still safe, you know, my lady.'

'Thank Heaven and the Great Genii[8] who watched over me!' ejaculated the Marchioness. 'Now, Mina, go to bed, as I am sure you must be tired. I can undress myself.'

Mina then left the room, and in a few minutes her young mistress, oppressed with grief and watching, was enjoying a temporary oblivion of her sorrows in the repose of sleep.

CHAPTER FOUR

She had scarcely rested three hours when Mina again stood by her bedside. 'My lady,' said she, 'will you rise now? The Marquis has sent up to say that breakfast is waiting.'

'What o'clock is it?' asked Marian.

'Nine, my lady.'

'Oh! then I will rise, of course. How provoking that he should have to wait for me!'

The Marchioness was soon dressed, as her attire in the morning is dictated by the very spirit of tasteful simplicity; and a few touches brought her soft, naturally curling glossy tresses into becoming order. When the business of the toilette was over, she proceeded to attend the Marquis. Her heart beat fast as she approached the breakfast room, for she had not seen him since the interview mentioned in one of my former chapters, when he left her in anger, sternly prohibiting any intercourse with Miss Foxley – and how had this prohibition been attended to?

Arthur, as she entered the apartment, was seated with his back to the door, engaged in the perusal of a newspaper. Her tread was too light to attract attention, and she feared to address him unspoken to, uncertain whether he had yet forgotten his wrathful mood, so she quietly took her seat at the table and began to arrange the material for breakfast.

The tinkle of porcelain and silver soon roused him; he looked up with a smile and said, 'Well, Marian, won't you bid me good morning? I hope you are not in a bad temper at being called out of your bed so early?'

'No, indeed, Arthur on the contrary. I am ashamed of myself for having made you wait so long. Forgive me, however, as I am not often so deficient in punctuality.'

'I'll consider about it,' replied he playfully. 'Perhaps your request may be granted, for I do not find myself inclined to be very angry on that score.'

My brother's breakfast is generally protracted to the space of about an hour and a half, as instead of eating straightforward, like other people, he sits maundering over the morning papers and, as my landlord says, taking a sup and a bite at intervals of about a quarter of an hour each. Some ladies of my acquaintance would raise a fine hubbub if they had to wait for their husbands such an unconscionable length of time; but the Marchioness of Douro, who considers herself honoured in being permitted to attend the beck of her lord and master when she has finished her own slight repast, usually takes up some piece of ornamental fancy-work and continues patiently plying the needle with her small, slight figures until the last leading article of the last newspaper is concluded.

This morning, her labour was interrupted by frequent and deep sighs. Every time one of these indications of grief escaped her lips, the Marquis, though unseen by his wife, just lifted his eyes from the paper and surveyed her with a most peculiar expression; and when they fell again on the speech or paragraph, he seemed for a moment rather engaged with his own thoughts than the sense of what he was reading. At length, like all sublunary things, Arthur's breakfast had an end; the service being cleared away and all set to rights by an attendant footman, Marian was about to leave the rooms in order to visit her nursery, when suddenly the Marquis rose, and coming close up to her, took her hand.

'Marian,' said he after a momentary silence, 'you look very pale this morning. What is the reason for it?'

'I – I – did not sleep very well last night,' stammered she, while her frame trembled like an aspen leaf.

'That is not all; it could not occasion this tremor. And what makes your hand turn so cold within mine?'

'I am sure I do not know,' replied Marian, endeavouring to force a smile; but the attempt only brought a tear into her dark blue eye.

The Marquis looked at her as if he would have pierced to the furthest recesses of her heart, and said in a low thrilling voice, 'Have you disobeyed my mandates? Have you seen that woman and are her chains again riveted round you?'

There was a pause. Marian seemed almost annihilated; the rapidly varying hue of her countenance proclaimed the violence of those emotions with which her soul was now rent. She could not answer, she could not even look up at her imperious lord, but stood voiceless and motionless like one petrified.

'It is well,' said he, dropping her hand and sternly folding his arms. 'I understand that silence. You have chosen to follow the direction of your own weak inclinations and to disregard my wishes. I have told you before that the consequence of such a line of conduct would be an immediate separation. It is my custom to make my words and deeds conformable; therefore, this very day and before three days elapse, the travelling carriage will be in readiness to take you to my father's country house in Wellington's Land. Goodbye. This is in all probability our last interview, for I cannot love a disobedient wife.'

'Arthur, my dearest Arthur, don't leave me thus! You would not think so hardly of me if you knew all!'

'Tell me all, then!' said he hastily, and taking his hand from the door lock, which he was just about to turn.

'I dare not!'

'And why?'

'Because I am bound by a promise not to consult you for a week; and at the end of that time all consultation will, I fear, be in vain, for then I must leave you for ever.'

The Marquis was going to answer, when the door opened and His Grace the Duke of Wellington entered. He halted, as Bobadil[9] would say, on the threshold, and after looking keenly from Arthur to Marian and noting the attitude and countenance of each, said in a quiet tone of enquiry, 'What ails you both? Have I arrived just in time to witness a slight specimen of matrimonial felicity, eh?'

There was no answer; the Marquis only moved away to a window and began to watch the clouds as they sailed slowly by. His Grace then addressed himself more particularly to the lady. 'What have you done, Marian,' said he, 'to bring that lowering and tempestuous cloud over your husband's countenance?'

Marian burst into tears. 'I did not mean to offend him,' sobbed she, 'but –'

'But what, love? I trust this is not unnecessary severity on his part.'

'No, no, no, he only wishes to know something which I cannot tell him.'

'And what is that something? Can you tell me?'

'Yes,' said the Marchioness, looking up, while a smile began to illumine her still glistening eyes. 'I think I will. Your Grace will know how to advise me better than anyone else, and I have not promised to keep it a secret from you.'

'Come then, child; sit down by me and let us hear this wonderful secret.'

Marian sat down beside the Duke as he desired her; for a little while she was silent and seemed to be collecting her faculties and summoning resolution for some great effort. The composure of resignation rather than peace at length over-spread her features, but there was still a wildness in her look and a tremble in her voice as she said, 'My lord Duke, I am not your son's wife, I am not Sir Alexander Hume's daughter.'

At these words the Marquis of Douro started as if he had received a shock of electricity. He turned round and would have spoken, but his father restrained him, saying, 'Hush, Arthur, not a word from your lips or I shall desire you to quit the room instantly. Now my love,' he continued, addressing Marian, 'explain to me in the first place how you are not my son's wife.'

'About five years ago,' replied she, 'a short time before my mother, or her whom until lately I considered as such, died, and when she was fast wasting under that languishing disease which at length destroyed her, I was one day summoned to her chamber. She was sitting up supported by pillows, and near the bedside stood Mr Hall, our private chaplain, Miss Foxley, my governess, whom Your Grace may perhaps remember to have seen,' (the Duke nodded assent) 'and Henry Percy, the youngest son of Lord Ellrington, whose country seat was situated not far from Badey Hall. He was a boy about my own age, and had been my playfellow as long as I could remember.

'"Marian," said my mother when I came to her, "you have often heard me speak of the late Lady Percy, have you not?" I said I had, and she went on, "She was my dearest friend. All her wishes are now sacred to me, and there is one of them which this day I desire to see fulfilled. One her deathbed, shortly after you and Henry were born, she expressed a wish that, in remembrance of our friendship, you should be united in case of your both arriving at years of discretion. I am now dying, and tomorrow Henry will depart on a voyage to a distant part of the world, whence he may never return. I should like, therefore, to see you betrothed now in my presence, and if my always hitherto dutiful daughter would render her mother's last moment happy, she will consent to bestow her hand on one who I doubt not will hereafter render her a happy wife."

'I could not refuse to comply with my dear mother's request, when I knew how soon the grave and coffin were to hide her forever from my sight; and besides, even had the powerful motive of obedience to her been absent, I could have found no excuse in my own inclinations to sanction a refusal: though I did not then know what love was, yet I had always liked Henry Percy, who was a handsome and affectionate boy, for his good nature and kind disposition. We accordingly pledged our faith before the chaplain and each gave the other a token by which, when we met again at some future period, we might recognise each other. The next day he set out on his long journey, and a few weeks after, my mother was carried to the tomb.

'Time passed on, and I heard nothing of Henry till the third year after his departure, when one morning Miss Foxley was looking over a newspaper in which she showed me a paragraph announcing the wreck of *The Mermaid*, the ship which Henry had sailed in, among some distant and unknown countries called the South Sea Islands, and the destruction of all her crew, including Lieutenant Percy, son of the celebrated Alexander Rogue. I mourned for Henry's death, but neither long nor bitterly. Absence had caused his image and the calm, childlike affection with which I viewed him to grow dim in my mind and memory.

'Twelve months after, I saw the Marquis; new feelings, passions which I had never till then experienced, arose in my heart. I need not tell Your Grace that all things were settled for my union with your son, when, in what must have appeared to you an unaccountably capricious manner, I suddenly stopped the preparations and declared that I never could consent to be his wife. I had, however, a reason, and one sufficiently conclusive. Three days before my marriage was to have taken place, and while Miss Foxley was engaged in making my bridal dress, she received a letter from a shipmate of Henry's with whom she was acquainted, declaring that the story of *The Mermaid*'s wreck was all false and that both vessel and crew were well and pursuing a prosperous voyage.

'You cannot, my lord, I think, blame me if after this, though with the greatest violence to my own feelings, I broke off all intercourse with your son. None can tell what I suffered when I saw him day by day pining for my sake, but Duty strongly pointed out to me the path which I ought to pursue, and I dared not turn aside. Your opinion of my caprice must have been confirmed, when after several months of steady rejection, I at once and suddenly yielded to his entreaties. There was a cause for this, but I scarcely dare tell it you lest you should suspect me of an inclination for romance.'

The Duke encouraged her to continue, and she went on. 'Late one calm summer's evening, I wandered out to a distant part of the grounds, and sitting down in a little wild alcove which was my favourite retreat, began sorrowfully to brood over the image of Arthur and the sad certainty that I should never be his. I thought and wept till it began to grow dark; and then, fearful of passing through the park at night and disturbing the deer and wild cattle from their slumbers, I rose to return and had advanced a little way up the forest walk where the alcove was erected, when a voice, faint and mournful, whispered my name. I turned and saw, standing under the arch I had just left, the dim figure of a man.

'"Who is there?" I asked in some alarm.

'Instead of answering, he glided towards me. I shrieked out. He beckoned me to be silent and said, in very hollow tones which I shudder even now to recollect, "Look at me, Marian, and know your Henry."

'Just then the moon broke from a cloud, and her light, falling through the branches, revealed to me a form and face which bore, indeed, a slight resemblance to Henry; but it was so changed and distorted that I should never have recognised it of my own accord. The hair and clothes were all wet and dripping, the eyes wide open but void of all expression save one of ghastliness, the face blue and livid and all the features swollen. I was too much appalled at this horrid change to answer, and he went on:

'"So I lie, Marian, among the Coral Islands of the South Sea. Listen not to deceivers, fear not that I shall return. Death and the waters of a vast deep chain me to my place; be happy and think of your first love no more." The wraith then walked into air before me, and filled with horror, I hastened back to the house.

'On arriving there, I related what I had seen to Miss Foxley. She strongly endeavoured to persuade me that it was all the fruit of my own excited imagination; but, finding my belief in the reality of the apparition fixed, and likewise my determination to act according to its counsel, she grew angry and left me, saying she prayed that if I did marry the Marquis, my repentance hereafter would be deep and bitter. Three weeks subsequent to this I was married. Arthur, shortly after our union, dismissed Miss Foxley, which I was very glad of, as her sullen looks and threatening words filled me with an undefined feeling of fear.

'Since that time I have received no intelligence of her till about two days ago, when the Marquis informed me that he had seen her in the city and warned me against holding any communication with her. The same day a letter was brought me from her, saying that if I did not wish the whole of a certain transaction to come out, I would condescend, Marchioness as I was, to visit my old governess at her lodgings in Harley Street. I went, for I dared not do otherwise, and there I saw that Henry Percy whom till then I had supposed buried in the sea.

'He was so changed, and looked so dark and wild and meagre, that at first I denied his identity; but I was soon but too well convinced by the production of that very token which five years since I had given him as a pledge of my eternal faith. He would have claimed his right over me that instant; by tears and entreaties I, however, gained a reprieve of a week, on condition that during that time I would not consult with my husband on the subject and that I would return to Harley Street next day in order to learn an important secret concerning myself.

'At the second interview, Miss Foxley informed me that I was not the daughter of Sir Alexander Hume!

'"Who, then?" I asked.

'"The late ladies Hume and Percy," she replied, "were, as you know, most intimate friends. As a sign of their love for and confidence in each other, they agreed, when you and Henry were born, to exchange children and each bring up the other's child as their own. The affair was managed so dexterously that none but myself knew anything of it; and till this moment you have looked up to Dr Hume as your father, when in reality no less a person than Lord Ellrington stands in that relation to you."

'This information affected me so deeply that I fainted. On recovering, I told Miss Foxley that, unless she could bring proof of her assertion, I should consider all I had just heard in the light of a malignant falsehood. She then informed me that there was a written agreement of the affair enclosed in a casket of Lady Percy's, which was fastened by a secret spring formed in a particular part, which she described to me; and that most probably, from the difficulty of discovering this spring, Lord Ellrington yet retained the box unopened.

'Half maddened by the idea of being that man's child whom of all others I most dreaded and detested, I went, scarcely knowing what I did, to Ellrington House. There, by entreaties, I prevailed on His Lordship to show me the casket. I opened it, found the fatal document, glanced over it, and in a moment of anguish, consumed it in the flame of a candle which stood on a table.

'Now, my lord,' she continued, 'you know all my secret, and may, if you can, fathom the depth and weigh the burden of that misery under which my reason at times seems to totter. I hate explanation, and therefore shall condense what I have further to say into as brief a space as possible.'

When Marian had finished, the Marquis asked her to describe to him the token by which she had recognised Henry Percy.

'It was,' replied she, 'a small gold ring with a crystal stone containing a little of my hair braided, and my name written on the inside.'

'The vile old witch!' exclaimed Arthur. 'She bought it in Lapis' shop, and that fellow whom you saw is no more the person you took him to be than I am. As for the tale about Lord Ellrington, I doubt not it is a scandalous lie, and so I'll make her confess before the day is at an end.'

He then rang the bell and ordered three or four of the servants to go immediately to Harley Street and take Miss

Foxley and whomever they might find with her into custody. They soon returned, accompanied by the governess and her male accomplice, whom my father and brother instantly recognised as Edward Percy, the well-known scamp and oldest brother to the youth whose character he had assumed. He unblushingly declared that his only motive for joining in the fraud was to extort a sum of money; and Miss Foxley, finding herself thus deserted by her assistant, confessed the falsity of all she had pretended and explained the mystery of the paper in the casket by saying that such an agreement had really existed between the Ladies Hume and Percy, but had never been put into practice on account of their husbands' refusing to consent.

My father then told her that if she wished to escape punishment for her wickedness, she must instantly leave Africa for some distant country and never set foot on its shores again. 'I give you your choice,' said the Duke, 'between two evils – exile or the pillory. Choose that which you consider the least.'

She chose the former, and was accordingly shipped off the next day. As for Edward Percy, my father gave him ten sovereigns for his candid confession and dismissed him well satisfied.

'Do you forgive my involuntary disobedience now, Arthur?' asked the once more happy Marian, when all was settled.

A smile and a kiss answered her more satisfactorily than words. And thus ends my Tale of the Secret.

Lily Hart

It was on the evening of the memorable sixteenth of March, the day of the Great Insurrection,[10] that Mrs Hart, a respectable widow lady, and her daughter Lily, sat by the parlour fireside of their quiet and modest mansion, situated in one of the remote suburbs of Verdopolis. They had passed the day in a state of the most intense and feverish anxiety, hourly expecting that the flames of war, which were raging with such virulence in other parts of the city, would spread to the obscure quarter in which they dwelt. Happily, however, about three o'clock p.m., the incessant thunder of distant artillery, which till then they had heard pealing from the far-off eastern division began to die away. The cloud of smoke which hung so gloomily between earth and heaven waxed less dense, the tumultuous roar of battle grew fainter, and intelligence soon arrived that the rebellion had at length been completely put down by Government.

Hours elapsed before the two terrified females could free themselves from the flutter of excitement in which they had been kept all day. But when night fell down and all continued quiet, when several fresh messengers confirmed the good news, and when many of those who had been engaged in the combat, returning to their homes, declared that the army of rebels was utterly cut off, they began to feel themselves reassured, and after bolting the doors and fastening the windows of the house, ventured for the first time since morning to partake of a slight meal, which Bessie, their only servant, had managed, though half dead with fear, to prepare. When it was concluded both drew near to the fire. As yet, they felt too unsettled to engage in their usual occupations of reading or sewing, but sat talking over the fearful events of the day and conjecturing the probable consequences of this unsuccessful attempt against good government. While they

49

were thus employed, Lily suddenly stopped short in the midst of a sentence she was uttering.

'Listen, Mama,' said she. 'Do you not hear a noise in the garden?'

Her mother listened. 'I do,' she replied. 'It sounds like the moan of someone in pain. Perhaps it may proceed from some poor wounded creature, and if so, it is our duty to assist him.'

With these words, she stepped to a little glass door which opened into the garden. Lily followed her mother. It was a clear and still night; the moon and stars were shining most brilliantly in a perfectly unclouded heaven, and their descending beams revealed the form of a human being stretched on the grass near a little wicket, which was open. Mrs Hart called to the prostrate figure, but received no answer. She then went up to him and took his hand. It was very cold; he had ceased moaning and now lay motionless.

'I fear he is dead,' said the benevolent lady, in a tone of compassion, 'but hasten, Lily, and tell Bessie to run instantly for the nearest surgeon.'

'I know something of the art of surgery,' said a voice close at hand, while a tall figure entered by the open wicket. 'And if my skill would be of any use, it is at your service, madam.'

'Who are you, sir?' asked she, in some alarm at this sudden intrusion.

'An officer in the Grand Army of Verdopolis, madam, and one whom no individual of the fair sex needs to fear.'

Encouraged by the soft and gentle accent in which the stranger spoke, she expressed her gratitude for his timely offer of assistance; and soon the wounded man was, with the additional aid of Bessie, conveyed into the snug little parlour and safely deposited on a sofa. As the candlelight fell on his pallid features, the officer uttered an exclamation of surprise.

'I know this person,' said he; 'he is my dearest friend. I trust to God he yet lives. If not, Africa has this day sustained a great loss.'

He then hastened to revive him by means of stimulants and cordial waters, which Mrs Hart liberally supplied. Gradually he returned to life, and on opening his eyes, stared wildly round and would have spoken, but his military medical attendant strictly forbade him to utter a word. On examination, his wound was found to consist in a bayonet stab in the right side; it was not deep, and most fortunately the vital parts remained uninjured.

'By what name shall I call your friend, sir?' asked Mrs Hart, when the wound was staunched and bandaged and the poor sufferer put to bed.

'Mr Seymour,' replied the officer, after a moment's consideration. 'And my name is Colonel Percival. If I could venture to urge so bold a request, madam, I should wish him to remain here till he is completely cured. I will be your guarantee for the reimbursement of such expenses as you may incur on his account.'

Mrs Hart assured him of her perfect willingness to permit the stranger's sojourn; and then, after promising to call again next morning, Colonel Percival took his leave.

'What a handsome man that officer is,' said Lily Hart when he was gone. 'I never saw such dark and sparkling eyes or such a magnificent form and face. But he looks very young to be a colonel.'

'He does, my dear,' replied her mother. 'Most probably, however, he is a scion of some noble family. At least, I should conjecture so from his lofty and patrician appearance; and they, you know, obtain preferment early.'

Days and weeks passed away, and Mr Seymour recovered rapidly under the treatment of his friend, who attended him with the most assiduous and constant care. The invalid's manners at first were not very prepossessing, in the opinion of his kind hostesses. He appeared cold and distant, and seemed to take all the attentions bestowed upon him as his right, but upon longer acquaintance this chilly reserve thawed almost entirely away. As his wound healed, he became more agreeable, and when, at length, he was able to leave his bedroom and sit in the little armchair by the parlour hearth, Lily wondered how she could ever have thought him either a plain or a proud man.

In person he was very tall, and so erect as to appear at times rather stiff and formal. His features were regularly formed, his forehead lofty and open, his eyes of a dark grey colour, deep-set and piercing. A general air of dignified gravity pervaded his whole countenance and, notwithstanding his youth, for he did not appear to be above twenty-five or six years of age, became him extremely well. He never laughed, but the contrast of his usual sobriety imparted an uncommon sweetness to his smile; but notwithstanding all of this, his disposition was evidently turned to a fondness for domestic life and female society. He would sit in a rustic seat in the garden, when he was able, weaving a garland of roses for the head of Lily or the neck of her favourite lap-dog. He constructed a pretty moss house and adorned it with shells and pebbles. At times, though not often, he would accompany Miss Hart's guitar with his powerful yet melodious voice, and regularly every morning, he gave her lessons in the Italian language, in which he appeared to be a proficient and which she was studying. Then in the evenings, when the curtains were let down and the fire burned bright, while the ladies sat at their needlework, Mr Seymour would read to them from some standard author, commenting on remarkable passages as he went on and illustrating such as were obscure, in language so lucid, so unassuming and at times so eloquent, as to give them a most exalted idea of his understanding. When he became earnest in conversation, which he often did if the subject interested him, his countenance grew very animated, his eyes sparkled and his words flowed forth with freedom, energy and even brilliancy.

Often when he was thus awakened, Lily would drop her work, gaze on him earnestly, and then, when the tide of inspired feeling gradually ebbed, and he returned to his customary calm and stately demeanour, she would reassume it with an involuntary sigh. Mrs Hart marked this and many other little indications of her daughter's growing regard for their guest. When Mr Seymour spoke, Lily was all rapt and earnest attention; when he was unusually grave, a sympathising sadness appeared on her face. If the slightest complaint of returning pain or weakness escaped him, she trembled lest he should relapse; and if a lighter tread or a gayer strain of conversation proclaimed improving health or spirits, her joy knew no bounds. All these tokens of incipient affection were noticed by the careful mother and occasioned her many an hour of anxious meditation, for though she could easily discern the state of her daughter's mind, yet that of the stranger defied her penetration. He was so sedate, so guarded, possessed such complete command over himself, that it was utterly impossible to read his thoughts in his countenance.

True, Lily was handsome enough to attract the attention of any man, and so my readers would have thought had they seen her. She was about eighteen years old, rather above than under the middle size, elegantly formed, with graceful rounded limbs and small fairylike face and hands. Her complexion was of a rich and sunny tone of colouring. Dark, bright eyes, softened by long, silken lashes, diffused a most fascinating expression over her sweet face, and harmonised well with the wild black curls which waved in such luxuriant clusters over her glowing vermilion cheeks. To these attractions were added a charming simplicity of dress and manner, all the refined accomplishments of a polite education and the more solid advantages of a useful one. Yet this lovely creature failed to excite any emotion in the, in this respect, almost stoical Mr Seymour, beyond what was indicated by an occasional fixed gaze, which was instantly withdrawn and compensated for by an additional degree of gravity and restraint.

In the space of two months he was, by dint of good nursing, restored to perfect health, but yet he did not seem willing to depart. One morning, while they were sitting at breakfast, Colonel Percival happened to call. After a little desultory conversation, he began to urge on his friend the necessity of returning to his family, who, he said, were beginning to be very anxious about him. Mr Seymour made no answer to his arguments, but appeared very loath to acknowledge their justice.

At length the Colonel said laughingly, 'Well, if you still refuse to quit your quarters, I shall begin to think someone has cast a spell round you. Perhaps my fair Lily here could furnish me with the name of the enchantress, if she would.'

A deep blush crimsoned the young philosopher's brow; he started up directly and exclaimed, 'I will go this instant, I will quit this peaceful retreat without delay. Mrs Hart, allow me to offer you a very slight compensation for your unwearied kindness and attention towards me.'

So saying, he tendered her a banknote of two hundred pounds. This, however, his disinterested hostess most promptly refused. In vain he implored her to accept it; she would not, and in the end he was compelled to return it to his pocketbook. Then, turning to Lily, he took her hand, pressed it gently, slipped off a valuable diamond ring, which decorated his little finger, placed it on hers, and with a faint, mournful farewell, abruptly left the house. Colonel Percival looked after him a moment with a significant smile, bowed gracefully to both the ladies, wished them a good morning, and departed.

A year elapsed, and during that little space of time poor Lily saw many and mighty changes. She had wept the loss of a loved and loving mother, whom a grave illness had in seven days' time carried to her grave; she had been left destitute by the failure of a banker in whose hands the whole of her small though competent fortune was lodged; and she had been forced to leave the house where she was born and brought up, and now resided in a humble dwelling containing only two apartments, where she endeavoured to support herself by manufacturing and selling ornamental articles such as screens, racks, etc. All day long she sat engaged in the production of the most beautiful and elegant forms, yet her utmost diligence could only procure her the means of a very scanty subsistence. In the meantime, not only desperation and grief for her parent's death but another deep-seated and hopeless sorrow greatly impaired her health. She grew thin and pale; her step lost its elasticity, her eye its lustre, her cheek its bloom, and in short she faded to the mere shadow of her former self.

One evening, after toiling ten weary hours over scraps of cardboard and shreds of gilt paper, sick at heart with her thankless labour, she rose, and wrapping herself in a large mantle, left her house to seek relaxation in a short walk.

Grateful was the freshness of the soft balmy summer's evening wind as it kissed her wasted cheek and played among her black, unbraided ringlets. The golden glory of a fast-westering sun lay on the distant harbour, brightened its busy shores and lit up with a warm glow the rocklike structure which soars from the centre of magnificent Verdopolis. Unconscious whither her way tended, she paced slowly on, gazing now at the dazzling west, now at the far-off hills which shone dimly visible in the excess of radiance which suffused them, and now at the dark blue waters of the seemingly waveless sea. Such an assemblage of lovely objects quickly calmed her griefs and excited in her mind a train of soothing meditations.

Ere long she was roused from her delicious reverie by a hum of human voices and a tread of passing footsteps, which warned her that she had left her own quiet quarter of the city and was entering upon a busier region. She looked up and saw that she was in the wide and splendid street called Ebor Terrace. Heaven-aspiring palaces of the most superb and imposing architecture rose on each side, and seemed in their princely pride to frown away any poor plebeian who might chance to fix his eye on them. This street, as my readers well know, is the Grand Corso of Verdopolis; and now, at the fashionable hour of sunset, it was crowded with hundreds of equestrians and pedestrians. Here groups of patrician beauties, lustrous in the fascination of bright eyes, lovely lips, beaming gems and nodding plumes, glided stately by, and as they went, a soft perfume and a sweet murmur of silver tones lingered on the breeze behind them. There a stately chariot with six or eight fiery horses passed full-speed like a rushing whirlwind, and everywhere the noble and the beautiful moved like beings of another sphere, seeming to disdain the ground on which they trod.

As poor Lily looked round on the glittering forms of life and splendour, not one of whom would condescend to cast a look or waste a thought on her, she felt a sensation of utter loneliness, and breathing a deep sigh, turned to depart. While she was hastily retracing her steps, she chanced to glance upwards at one of the majestic edifices frowning above her and saw, seated at an open window and gazing pensively at the brilliant crowds beneath, the well-remembered form of Mr Seymour. At this unexpected sight, a smothered exclamation of joyful surprise burst from Lily's lips and a radiant light sparkled in her dark eye. She stood transfixed for a moment, and while yet lost in wonder and delight, he raised his eyes and they fell on her. Blushing deeply, she hung down her head and covered her face with her hands; when she looked again the window was closed and the welcome vision departed.

'Cruel man,' thought she, while a shower of unbidden tears gushed forth. 'He might have spoken one little word to me, were it only for the sake of my mother's kindness.'

The recollection of her mother determined Lily to visit the grave where her beloved ashes reposed, and with the tardy tread of sorrow she took the way to St Michael's Cemetery. Twilight had quenched the glory of the setting sun in soft and silent shades ere she reached that huge wilderness of tombs, and a pale crescent moon was gilding the gloomy groves of gigantic cypress trees as she sat down near an upright headstone of grey marble, which stood close under the lofty southern wall. Utterly unbroken was the frozen hush which hung over that city of the dead. No step, no voice waked an echo among the silent tombs, but soon the cathedral clock tolled the hour of vespers, and then there came floating on the night air the swell of the solemn organ from the holy minster, which stood bathed in hoary moonbeams not far distant, and the sublime sound of a sacred song. As the chant died away, Lily took up the tune and sang mournfully the following stanzas:

Dark is the mansion of the dead,
Dark, desolate and still;
Around it dwells a solemn dread,
Within a charnel chill.

O Mother! Does thy spirit rest
In fairer worlds than ours?
'Mid tranquil valleys ever-blest,
And ever-blooming bowers?

I trust it doth, for thy pale clay
Hath found no fair abode,
Shut from the happy light of day,
Pressed by the cold earth's load.

Yet Mother! I would rest with thee
In thy long dreamless sleep.
Though dread its mute solemnity,
All voiceless, still and deep.

And I would rest my weary head
Upon thy lifeless breast,
Nor feel one shuddering thrill of dread
At what my temples prest.

Earth is a dreary void to me,
Heaven is a cloud of gloom.
Then Mother! let me sleep with thee,
Safe in thy stilly tomb.

She ceased, and throwing herself on the grassy grave, wept and sobbed bitterly. When this paroxysm of grief subsided, she rose, and was preparing to leave the cemetery, when a tall and dark figure glided from an adjoining cypress grove and stood before her. Overcome with terror at this unexpected apparition, she shrieked aloud.

'Does Miss Hart fear him whose life she saved?' said a deep calm voice.

Lily answered not, but seized with sudden faintness, sank on a stone which stood near. The stranger seated himself beside her and took her passive hand. 'Has my Lily forgotten the ungrateful Seymour?' he asked in soothing accents.

'No! Never! Never!' was her enthusiastic reply. 'Nor will I, till death separates me from all mental associations.'

'From what I have just heard,' said he, 'you have lost your earthly protector and are now left desolate in the world.'

'I am,' replied she briefly.

He paused a moment and then said, 'Lily, you have doubtless by this time concluded that I have lost all recollection of you and your household, but it is not so. I have striven indeed to forget you, laboured night and day to erase the impress of your too-dear image from my mind. To this end I have sought the drawing-room and the ballroom, in order to find some form of superior loveliness, some mind of higher excellence, than those which haunted me like a heavenly vision. But in vain. Not one could I discover amongst all the fairest and noblest of the land to vie with my peerless, my lovely Lily. At length, unable any longer to live without you, I determined, despite of foolish prejudice and family pride, to seek out the poor widow's daughter and gain her consent to a private union. With this resolution, I went about six months since to your house in the eastern suburbs, but it was empty and none knew whither you were gone. Since that time I have sought you, but in vain, till this evening, when I was gazing at the groups in Ebor Terrace, my eye rested on the long-desired form. I immediately quitted the house where I was, watched what way you took, followed you hither. And now, Miss Hart, will you be my wife or not? Say yes and you make a fellow creature happy for life; say no and you pronounce the death doom of one who never wronged you.'

After such an appeal, who could have uttered the cold and chilling negation? Lily could not; she saw at her feet the grave, the philosophical Mr Seymour, he who seemed to have subdued all the turbulent passions which agitate other men; she beheld him changed for her sake into a mere mortal lover; she heard him declare that his life's happiness depended on her decision; and she murmured a faint and faltering 'Yes!'

'Bless you, my dearest!' exclaimed he with energy, while he snatched her hand and pressed it passionately to his lips. 'Bless you for that little word! You are now mine and mine alone, and nothing save death shall divide us.' After a pause, he continued in his usual composed and deliberate manner. 'Circumstances, Miss Hart, which I cannot now explain to you render it imperative that our union should be strictly private. Do you agree to this?'

'I do,' she replied, for having unconditionally yielded the grand point, she could not now hesitate about trifles.

'Meet me, then,' proceeded Mr Seymour, 'tomorrow night at this hour in this place.'

She consented, and after one long and fervent embrace they parted. Some of my readers will doubtless consider that this was an imprudent transaction on the part of Lily, but let them remember that she loved Mr Seymour more than her life, that besides him there was not a creature on earth in whom she could centre her stock of warm affections, and that she was a young and inexperienced girl who had not yet completed her nineteenth year.

The whole of the next day Lily employed in making her bridal attire, and when it began to grow dark she dressed herself in it. It was a gown of a dark-coloured silk such as suited well with her complexion, ornamented here and there with small knots of pink ribbon. A larger bow of the same material bound up the rich jetty tresses which otherwise would have hung lower than her waist and made them form a natural coronet on the top of her head. Thus simply arrayed she looked most lovely; excitement had restored the bright rose to her cheek and the lustrous light to her eye. And when, wrapped in her dark mantle, she again passed over Ebor Terrace, there was none amongst all the hundreds there whose tread was so bounding and elastic as her own.

The crescent moon was again rising when she entered St Michael's Cemetery. A gusty, hollow-toned wind waved the great arms of the cypress trees as they stood like swart giants rising darkly against the twilight sky, and the last swell of the vesper organ was dying in the domed cathedral. Solemn and mournful were the sights and sounds of that darkling hour, but her buoyant spirits resisted the gloomy impression they were calculated to make, and full of happy anticipation she sought her mother's tomb. Her heart bounded as she saw a tall figure standing beside it, but on drawing nearer she perceived that it was not her lover but a military officer dressed in uniform; his sword and steel-clasped belt sparkled in the moonlight, and as he paced slowly to and fro with measured step he hummed the fragment of a merry march. Filled with dismay, she was about to retreat, when he suddenly raised his head and exclaimed, 'Is that you, Miss Hart?'

In the pronunciation of these words, Lily instantly recognised the deep melody of Colonel Percival's peculiarly fascinating voice, and the stranger's face being now turned to the light, she likewise knew the statue-like and noble beauty of his features. Now Lily had always admired the Colonel because he was a handsome and graceful man, but she feared him likewise on account of a certain lofty imperiousness in his manner and in the expression of his bright and bold dark eyes. His behaviour to her mother and herself had ever been perfectly kind and gentle, but there was a certain air of condescension mixed with it which, whenever she conversed with him, used to impress her with an indescribable feeling of awe. It was, therefore, with considerable misgiving and in a very timid tone that she answered his question in the affirmative.

'Do not be afraid, fair Lily,' said he encouragingly. 'I am here on behalf of my friend, Mr Seymour, who was prevented himself from coming to meet you by urgent business, any neglect of which would have excited enquiry and perhaps discovery, in which case the happiness he has so much at heart would infallibly have been snatched away from him at the moment of its completion. I hope you will not refuse to allow me to act as his substitute.'

Lily had gone too far to retreat, and she was therefore reluctantly compelled to accept the gay young officer as a conductor. When she had signified that she was ready to follow him, he uttered a shrill whistle, and immediately a splendid carriage dashed through the open gates of the cemetery. Having assisted her to enter it and placed himself by her side, he gave the word of departure, and off they rolled with the celerity of lightning.

The carriage blinds being down, Lily could not discern which way they went, but after an hour's rapid driving, the vehicle suddenly drew up and Colonel Percival informed her that she must now alight. On getting out she saw before her the pillared entrance of a vast park. A footman unfolded the gates, and her guide, drawing her arm through his, proceeded to follow the carriage road till they came in sight of a most extensive and magnificent mansion, or rather palace, whose white marble columns and turrets were all gleaming with softest radiance in the tranquil moonbeams. He then turned, crossed an angle of the park and, opening a small arched door which was formed in a lofty wall by which this portion of the grounds was bounded, they entered a large garden. After threading their way through long dark alleys through whose bowery arches scarcely a ray of light found ingress, and crossing open parterres where the closed and drooping blossoms and variegated green leaves were all wet and glittering with the tears of night, they at length reached a small chapel or oratory situated in the midst of a great wilderness of tall and fragrant flowering shrubs.

'Now,' whispered the Colonel, as they passed under the fretted porch and up the long echoing aisle, 'Now, fair Lily, I have discharged my trust and shall yield you to better hands.'

'And you have discharged it well,' said the voice of Mr Seymour, issuing from a neighbouring aisle. 'Adrian, I thank you, but do not depart till you have seen the indissoluble knot tied.'

He consented to remain in order to witness their union, and all three proceeded towards the altar, where a clergyman of a remarkably grave and venerable aspect stood ready in gown and cassock. In another quarter of an hour Lily Hart had changed her name and pledged her faith for life.

When the marriage ceremony was over, Percival took his friend's hand, warmly wished him joy, bade him farewell, and, after respectfully saluting the bride, departed.

'Now, my own dear Lily,' said Mr Seymour, turning to his wife, 'we must leave Verdopolis without delay, if you do not already feel too much fatigued.'

Lily assured him that she was not at all tired, and leaving the chapel they returned to the park gate, where the carriage still awaited their arrival.

All night long their journey continued, and at last, just about sunrise, Mr Seymour lifted one of the carriage blinds and bade his wife look out. She did so, and her eye beheld one of the fairest and most fertile scenes imagination can conceive. Emerald-green meadows stretched on every side, spotted here and there with tall, spreading forest trees and watered by a broad and placid river on whose banks, facing the east and bathed in the rosy light of early day, there appeared a small and elegant villa surrounded by a lawn and gardens and backed by a grove of tall young elm trees, whose branches, as they were shaken by the sweet morning wind, let fall a shower of dew on the clustering vines and roses which clung to its roof and sides.

'What a lovely place,' said Lily. 'I should like to live there.'

'Your wish is granted, my love,' replied her husband, 'for that is your destined place of abode.'

And for three years Lily dwelt in this peaceful little paradise, in the midst of as perfect happiness as it is possible for mortal man or woman to enjoy. Surrounded by all the elegancies and comforts of life, blessed ere long by a beautiful and healthy boy, cherished by an affectionate and tender husband whose mild philosophical manners and calm, deep attachment never lost either their charm or their strength, who could be happy if she was not? Yet there were one or two little circumstances which somewhat disturbed her felicity. In the first place, the mystery of their clandestine marriage still remained unsolved; she did not yet properly know who her husband was; she had never seen one member of his family or even heard him mention them. His anxiety to keep her in perfect seclusion was evident; he never once permitted her to visit Verdopolis, and no guest with the exception of Colonel Percival was ever allowed to enter Elm Grove Villa. In the second place, she was often for weeks together deprived of Mr Seymour's own society. He seldom upon an aggregate spent more than the fourth part of the year with her, the rest being devoted to important business in the city. It is true, the brevity and the fewness of his visits rendered them more delightful, but notwithstanding this, she could not help occasionally expressing a wish that she might see more of one so justly dear to her.

One evening at the commencement of the fourth year of her marriage, she, her husband and Colonel Percival (whom Lily had learnt to regard not only without fear but with feelings of the warmest and purest friendship) were all assembled in the villa drawing-room. It was a wild and tempestuous night. Torrents of rain dashed incessantly against the windows; a gusty wind swept in fierce but wailing howls through the crashing elm grove; and every now and then its melancholy voice was mingled with the dull muttering of distant thunder. This war of elements without the villa, however, seemed only to increase the cheerfulness of the party within. Lily, seated at her harp, was uttering tones melodious enough, one would have thought, to have charmed the wildest storm that ever rushed with blast and thunder through the midnight heavens. Her husband bent over her, listening in rapt attention to the sweetness of her voice and harp. As for Colonel Percival, he was busily engaged with his pet, little Augustus Seymour, now tossing him in his arms, now dancing before his dazzled eyes a glittering watch and chain, and then again teaching him how to handle and cock a small pistol which he loaded with powder and discharged once or twice, while the bold, spirited child, instead of being terrified, clapped his hands and chuckled with delight at every explosion.

'Colonel,' said Lily, rising when she had ceased her song and advancing towards him with a smile, 'you will spoil my child by your too-great indulgence. Already he is getting as wilful and unmanageable as – as –'

'As myself, madam, you would say,' interrupted the Colonel, laughing. 'Be it so, I have no desire to see him otherwise. If he could unite a little of my impetuosity with his father's wisdom, he would be perfect, you know.'

She was going to reply in the same half-playful, half-serious strain, when a tremendous peal of thunder burst just over their heads.

'The storm increases,' observed Mr Seymour. 'How dreadful must be the situation of those who are exposed to its fury.'

He had scarcely uttered these words when the sound of approaching carriage wheels, followed by a violent ringing of the doorbell and a correspondingly vigorous agitation of the knocker, proclaimed that there were persons without who suffered even now the pitiless drenching of the tempest. Directly after, a servant opened the door and announced that a gentleman and two ladies had arrived in an open chariot and requested shelter till the storm should pass over.

'Show them into the dining-room,' said Mr Seymour.

'The fire is gone out in that room, sir,' replied the servant, 'and they are dripping wet.'

'Well, then, bring them here. I suppose, Adrian,' looking towards the Colonel, 'they are not persons who know anything of us, so it does not much signify.'

Steps were now heard on the staircase, the door was again flung open, and there entered first a tall, perpendicular, rigid-looking old gentleman of about sixty, with high bald forehead trimmed with a fringe of silver hair, aquiline nose and very keen, piercing grey eyes. Then a lady who had passed the meridian of life but still retained in her benevolent countenance and mild blue eyes the remains of what had once been sur-passing loveliness, and lastly a tall, slender and beautiful girl. Both the ladies were enveloped in large dark velvet mantles lined with costly ermine; these rich garments were wet through and clung round them as if they had been flimsy taffeta.

The effect which the appearance of this imposing trio produced upon Percival and Seymour seemed very unaccount-able to Lily. The former sprang up, exclaiming with an astonished smile, 'Lord bless me, the day of discovery is come at last, the hour when the secrets of all hearts shall be revealed. But never mind, John, stand it out boldly like a man. Flinch not, lie not, but make a clean bosom and take what shall come thereafter.'

Mr Seymour did seem greatly to need this advice. He had stood up and with folded arms and an air of cool determination had taken his station just opposite the door.

'What means all this, my lord Marquis?' asked the old gentleman, looking sternly at Colonel Percival. 'Why do I find you and my son here, and who is this woman?'

'That woman,' replied Seymour, in a firm but respectful tone, 'that woman, royal father, is my dear wife Lily, Marchioness of Fidena. I crowned her with my coronet three years since, and there by her side stands my son and your grandson, John Augustus Sneaky.'

The appearance of a thousand disembodied spirits could not have stricken the royal party with more mute astonishment than did this simple piece of intelligence. At length, after gazing at his son silently for some minutes, the monarch Alexander spoke:

Do not think to impose on me thus,' he said. 'That presumptuous woman shall return immediately to her native obscurity, from which you have so wickedly raised her, unless you can produce the fullest proof of your marriage and unless that marriage was solemnised by the Chief Prelate, for no humbler priest can lawfully wed a prince of the blood.'

'I can bear witness to Your Majesty,' replied Colonel Percival, or as we must now call him, the Marquis of Douro, for such he really was, 'that about this time three years since, John, Prince of Fidena, was united to Lily Hart by Gravey, the Metropolitan Archbishop himself, before the high altar of the private chapel situated in the gardens which surround your imperial palace on the banks of the Niger, I standing by and giving away the bride with my own hands.'

A dark and ominous flush covered Alexander's haughty brow when he heard this pronounced by the unabashed Marquis in a tone of the most perfect and easy nonchalance. What he would have said or done I know not, but just as he was about to speak, the Queen and her eldest daughter Lady Edith (my readers will have already recognised these exalted personages in the two females who accompanied him) flung themselves at his feet and implored him to forgive what could not now be undone and to receive once more to his paternal favour the son who till now had never offended him. Lily, trembling like an aspen leaf and pale as her floral namesake, joined her tears to their entreaties. Alexander, however, remained quite unmoved by their supplications and would probably have given free vent to the indignation which boiled within him, had not the Marquis of Douro stepped up to him and whispered in a low, emphatic tone:

'Monarch of the mountains, you may indeed cast this son away, but where will you turn to find another who shall be more worthy to inherit your crown and throne? Nowhere; therefore royalty must depart from your line and the sceptre pass into the hands of aliens.'

'You have spoken truth,' replied the Twelve[11] after a pause. 'Therefore, Prince John, I forgive you, but take notice it is not from the weakness of compassion, but merely because necessity compels me to it. Had I another son who was yet guiltless of any such daring act of disobedience, I would disown you, your wife and child instantly and for ever.'

Prince John made no answer to this speech of his royal father's; he only bowed low, and raising his kneeling wife, said, with a pride almost equal to that of Alexander himself, 'Now, my Lily, you shall appear in the circles for which Nature designed you, and if anyone dare breathe a word of scorn against you or yours, by Heaven, that word shall be his last.'

On Monday last, the Marchioness of Fidena made her first public appearance in Verdopolis at a grand ball given on the occasion at Elimbos Palace, the residence of the King, her father-in-law. I saw her and can safely state that Lily Hart, the widow's daughter, is worthy for grace and beauty to rank with the noblest-born and fairest of Verdopolis.

Albion and Marina[12]

CHAPTER ONE

There is a certain sweet little pastoral village in the south of England with which I am better acquainted than most men. The scenery around it possesses no distinguished characteristic of romantic grandeur and wildness that might figure to advantage in a novel, to which title this brief narrative sets up no pretension. Neither rugged lofty rocks, nor mountains dimly huge mark with frowns the undisturbed face of nature, but little peaceful valleys, low hills crowned with wood, murmuring cascades and streamlets, richly cultivated fields, farmhouses, cottages and a wide river form all the scenic features, and every hamlet has one or more great men.

This had one and he was 'na sheepshank'[13]. Every ear in the world had heard of his fame, and every tongue could bear testimony to it. I shall name him the Duke of Strathelleraye,[14] and by that name the village was likewise denominated.

For more than thirty miles around every inch of ground belonged to him and every man was his retainer.

The magnificent villa, or rather palace, of this noble, stood on an eminence, surrounded by a vast park and the embowering shade of an ancient wood, proudly seeming to claim the allegiance of all the countryside.

The mind, achievements and character of its great possessor, must not, *can* not, be depicted by a pen so feeble as mine; for though I could call filial love and devoted admiration to my aid, yet both would be utterly ineffective.

Though the Duke seldom himself came among his attached vassals, being detained elsewhere by important avocations, yet his lady the Duchess resided in the castle constantly. Of her I can only say that she was like an earthly angel. Her mind was composed of charity, beneficence, gentleness and sweetness. All, both old and young, loved her; and the blessings of those that were ready to perish came upon her evermore.

His Grace had also two sons, who often visited Strathelleraye. Of the youngest, Lord Cornelius,[15] everything is said when I inform the reader that he was seventeen years of age, grave, sententious, stoical, rather haughty and sarcastic, of a fine countenance, though somewhat swarthy; that he had long thick hair, black as the hoody's wing,[16] and liked nothing so well as to sit in moody silence musing over the vanity of human affairs, or improving and expanding his mind by the abstruse study of the higher branches of mathematics and that sublime science, astronomy.

The eldest son, Albion, Marquis of Tagus, is the hero of my present tale. He had entered his nineteenth year, his stature was lofty, his form equal in the magnificence of its proportions to that of Apollo Belvedere[17]. The bright wealth and curls of his rich brown hair waved over a forehead of the purest marble in the placidity of its unveined whiteness. His nose and mouth were cast in the most perfect mould. But I never saw anything to equal his eye! Oh! I could have stood riveted with the chains of admiration gazing for hours upon it! What clearness, depth and lucid transparency in those large orbs of radiant brown! And the fascination of his smile was irresistible, though seldom did that sunshine of the mind break through the thoughtful and almost melancholy expression of his noble features. He was a soldier, captain in the Royal Regiment of Horse Guards, and all his attitudes and actions were full of martial grace. His mental faculties were in exact keeping with such an exterior, being of the highest order; and though not like his younger brother, wholly given up to study, yet he was well versed in the ancient languages, and deeply read in the Greek and Roman classics, in addition to the best works in the British, German and Italian tongues.

Such was my hero. The only blot I was able to discover in his character was that of a slight fierceness or impetuosity of temper, which sometimes carried him beyond bounds, though at the slightest look or word of command from his father he instantly bridled his passion and became perfectly calm.

No wonder the Duke should be, as he was, proud of such a son.

CHAPTER TWO

About two miles from the castle there stood a pretty house, entirely hid from view by a thick forest, in a glade of which it was situated.

Behind it was a smooth lawn fringed with odiferous shrubs, and before it a tasteful flower garden.

This was the abode of Sir Alured Angus, a Scotchman, who was physician to His Grace, and though of gentlemanly manners and demeanour, yet harsh, stern and somewhat querulous in countenance and disposition.

He was a widower, and had but one child, a daughter, whom I shall call Marina, which nearly resembles her true name.

No wild rose blooming in solitude, or bluebell peering from an old wall, ever equalled in loveliness this flower of the forest. The hue of her cheek would excel the most delicate tint of the former, even when its bud is just opening to the breath of summer, and the clear azure of her eyes would cause the latter to appear dull as a dusky hyacinth. Also, the silken tresses of her hazel hair, straying in light ringlets down a neck and forehead of snow, seemed more elegant than the young tendrils of a vine. Her dress was almost Quaker-like in its simplicity. Pure white or vernal green were the colours she constantly wore, without any jewels save one row of pearls round her neck. She never stirred beyond the precincts of the wooded and pleasant green lane which skirted a long cornfield near the house. There, on warm summer evenings, she would ramble and linger, listening to the woodlark's song, and occasionally join her own more harmonious voice to its delightful warblings.

When the gloomy days and regrets of autumn and winter did not permit these walks, she amused herself with drawing (for which she had an exact taste), playing on the harp, reading the best English, French and Italian works (all which languages she understood) in her father's extensive library, and sometimes a little light needlework.

Thus in a state of almost perfect seclusion (for seldom had she even Sir Alured's company, as he generally resided in London), she was quite happy, and reflected with innocent wonder on those who could find pleasure in the noisy delights of what is called 'fashionable society'.

One day, as Lady Stratelleraye was walking in the wood, she met Marina, and on learning who she was, being charmed with her beauty and sweet manners, invited her to go on the morrow to the castle. She did so, and there met the Marquis of Tagus. He was even more surprised and pleased with her than the Duchess, and when she was gone he asked his mother many questions about her, all of which she answered to his satisfaction.

For some time afterwards he appeared listless and abstracted. The reader will readily perceive that he had, to use a cant phrase, fallen in love. Lord Cornelius, his brother, warned him of the folly of doing so; but instead of listening to his sage admonitions, he first strove to laugh, and then, frowning at him, commanded silence.

In a few days he paid a visit to Oakwood House (Sir Alured's mansion), and after that became more gloomy than ever. His father observed this; and one day, as they were sitting alone, remarked it to Albion, adding that he was fully acquainted with the reason. Albion reddened but made no answer.

'I am not, my son,' continued the Duke, 'opposed to your wishes, though certainly there is a considerable difference of rank between yourself and Marina Angus. But that difference is compensated by the many admirable qualities she possesses.'

On hearing these words, Arthur – Albion, I mean – started up, and throwing himself at his father's feet, poured forth his thanks in terms of glowing gratitude, while his fine features, flushed with excitation, spoke even more eloquently than his eloquent words.

'Rise, Albion!' said the Duke. 'You are worthy of her and she of you; but both are yet too young. Some years must elapse before your union takes place. Therefore exert your patience, my son.'

Albion's joy was slightly damped by this news, but his thankfulness and filial obedience, as well as love, forced him to acquiesce; immediately after, he quitted the room and took his way to Oakwood House. There he related the circumstance to Marina, who, though she blushed incredulously, yet felt as much gladness and as great a relief from doubt – almost amounting to despair – as himself.

CHAPTER THREE

A few months afterwards, the Duke of Strathelleraye determined to visit that wonder of the world, the great city of Africa, the Glass Town – of whose splendour, magnificence and extent, strength and riches, occasional tidings came from afar, wafted by breezes of the ocean to Merry England. But to most of the inhabitants of that little isle it bore the character of a dream or gorgeous fiction. They were unable to comprehend how mere human beings could construct fabrics of such marvellous size and grandeur as many of the public buildings were represented to be, and as to the Tower of all the Nations, few believed in its existence. It seemed as the cities of old: Nineveh or Babylon with the temples of their gods, Ninus or Jupiter Belus, and their halls of Astarte and Semele.[18] These most people believe to be magnified by the dim haze of intervening ages, and the exaggerating page of history through which medium we behold them.

The Duke, as he had received many invitations from the Glass Townians, who were impatient to behold one whose renown had spread so far, and who likewise possessed vast dominions near the African coast, informed his lady, the Marquis of Tagus and Lord Cornelius, that in a month's time he should take his departure with them, and that he should expect them all to be prepared at that period, adding that when they returned, Marina Angus should be created Marchioness of Tagus.

Though it was a bitter trial to Albion to part with one to whom he was now so entirely devoted, yet, comforted by the last part of his father's speech, he obeyed without murmuring.

On the last evening of his stay in Strathelleraye, he took a sad farewell of Marina, who wept as if hopeless. But suddenly restraining her griefs she looked up, with her beautiful eyes irradiated by a smile that like a ray of light illuminated the crystal tears, and whispered, 'I shall be happy when you return.'

Then they parted, and Albion, during his voyage over the wide ocean, often thought for comfort on her last words. It is common superstition that the words uttered by a friend on separating are prophetic, and these certainly portended nothing but peace.

CHAPTER FOUR

In due course of time they arrived at the Glass Town, and were welcomed with enthusiastic cordiality. After the Duke had visited his kingdom, he returned to the chief metropolis, and established his residence there at Salamanca Palace.

The Marquis of Tagus, from the noble beauty of his person, attracted considerable attention wherever he went, and in a short period he had won and attached many faithful friends of the highest rank and abilities. From his love of elegant literature and the fine arts in general, painters and poets were soon among his warmest admirers. He himself possessed a sublime genius, but as yet its full extent was unknown to him.

One day, as he was meditating alone on the world of waters that rolled between him and the fair Marina, he determined to put his feelings on paper in a tangible shape that he might hereafter show them to her when anticipation had given place to fruition. He took his pen, and in about a quarter of an hour had completed a brief poem of exquisite beauty. The attempt pleased him and soothed the anguish that lingered in his heart. It likewise gave him an insight into the astonishing faculties of his own mind, and a longing for immortality, an ambition of glory, seized him. [...][19] tragedy, wreathed the laurels of fame round his brow, and his after-productions, each of which seemed to excel the other, added new wreaths to those which already beautified his temples.

I cannot follow him in the glory of his literary career, nor even mention so much as the titles of his various works. Suffice it to say he became one of the greatest poets of the age, and one of the chief motives that influenced him in his exertions for renown was to render himself worthy to possess such a treasure as Marina. She, in whatever he was employed, was never out of his thoughts, and none had he as yet beheld among all the ladies of the Glass Town – though rich, titled and handsome strove by innumerable arts to gain his favour – whom he could even compare with her.

CHAPTER FIVE

One evening Albion was invited to the house of Earl Cruachan, where was a large party assembled. Among the guests was one lady apparently about twenty-five or twenty-six years of age. In figure she was very tall, and both it and her face were of a perfectly Roman cast. Her features were regularly and finely formed, her full and brilliant eyes jetty black, as were the luxuriant tresses of her richly curled hair. Her dark glowing complexion was set off by a robe of crimson velvet trimmed with ermine, and a nodding plume of black ostrich feathers added to the imposing dignity of her appearance.

Albion, notwithstanding her unusual comeliness, hardly noticed her till Earl Cruachan rose and introduced her to him as the Lady Zelzia Ellrington.[20] She was the most learned and noted woman in Glass Town, and he was pleased with the opportunity of seeing her. For some time she entertained him with a discourse of the most lively eloquence, and indeed Madame de Staël[21] herself could not have gone beyond Lady Zelzia in the conversational talent. On this occasion she exerted herself to the utmost, as she was in the presence of so distinguished a man, and one whom she seemed ambitious to please.

At length one of the guests asked her to favour the company with a song and tune on the grand piano. At first she refused, but, on Albion seconding the request, rose, and taking from the drawing-room table a small volume of poems, opened it at one by the Marquis of Tagus. She then set it to a fine air and sang as follows, while she skilfully accompanied her voice upon the instrument:

I think of thee when the moonbeams play
On the placid water's face;
For thus thy blue eyes' lustrous ray
Shone with resembling grace.

I think of thee when the snowy swan
Glides calmly down the stream;
Its plumes the breezes scarcely fan,
Awed by their radiant gaze.

For thus I've seen the loud winds hush
To pass thy beauty by,
With soft caress and playful rush
'Mid thy bright tresses fly.

And I have seen the wild birds sail
In rings thy head above,
While thou hast stood like lily pale
Unknowing of their love.

Oh! for the day when once again
Mine eyes will gaze on thee,
But an ocean vast, a sounding main,
An ever-howling sea,
Roll on between
With their billows green,
High-tost tempestuously.

This song had been composed by Albion soon after his arrival at the Glass Town. The person addressed was Marina. The full rich tones of Lady Zelzia's voice did ample justice to the subject, and he expressed his sense of the honour she had done him in appropriate terms.

When she had finished, the company departed, for it was then rather late.

CHAPTER SIX

As Albion pursued his way homewards, he began insensibly to meditate on the majestic charms of Lady Zelzia Ellrington, and to compare them with the gentler ones of Marina Angus. At first he could hardly tell which to give the preference to, for though he still almost idolised Marina, yet an absence of four years had considerably deadened his remembrance of her person.

While he was thus employed, he heard a soft but mournful voice whisper, 'Albion!'

He turned hastily round, and saw the form of the identical Marina at a little distance, distinctly visible by the moonlight.

'Marina! My dearest Marina!' he exclaimed, springing towards her, while joy unutterable filled his heart. 'How did you come here? Have the angels in heaven brought you?'

So saying he stretched out his hand, but she eluded his grasp, and slowly gliding away, said, 'Do not forget me; I shall be happy when you return.'

Then the apparition vanished. It seemed to have appeared merely to assert her superiority over her rival, and indeed the moment Albion beheld her beauty he felt that it was peerless. But now wonder and perplexity took possession of his mind. He could not account for this vision except by the common solution of supernatural agency, and that ancient creed his enlightened understanding had hitherto rejected until it was forced upon him by this extraordinary incident. One thing there was, however, the interpretation of which he thought he could not mistake, and that was the repetition of her last words: 'I shall be happy when you return.' It showed that she was still alive, and that which he had seen could not be her wraith. However, he made a memorandum of the day and hour, namely, the 18th of June, 1815, twelve o'clock at night.

From this time the natural melancholy turn of his disposition increased, for the dread of her death before he should return was constantly before him; the ardency of his adoration and desire to see her again redoubled. At length, not being able any longer to bear his misery, he revealed it to his father, and the Duke, touched with his grief and the fidelity of his attachment, gave him full permission to visit England and bring back Marina with him to Africa.

CHAPTER SEVEN

I need not trouble the reader with a minute detail of the circumstances of Albion's voyage, but shall pass on to what happened after he arrived in England.

It was a fair evening in September 1815 when he reached Strathelleraye. Without waiting to enter the halls of his fathers, he proceeded immediately to Oakwood House. As he approached it, he almost sickened, when, for an instant, the thought that she might be no more passed across his mind. But summoning hope to his aid, and resting on her golden anchor, he passed up the lawn and gained the glass doors of the drawing-room.

As he drew near a sweet symphony of harp music swelled on his ear. His heart bounded within him at the sound. He knew that no fingers but hers could create those melodious tones, with which now blended the harmony of a sweet and sad, but well-known voice. He lifted the vine branch that shaded the door and beheld Marina, more beautiful, he thought, than ever, seated at her harp, sweeping with her slender fingers the quivering chords.

Without being observed by her, as she had her face turned from him, he entered; sitting down, he leaned his head on his hand, and, closing his eyes, listened with feelings of overwhelming transport to the following words:

Long my anxious ear hath listened
For the step that ne'er returned;
And my tearful eye hath glistened,
And my heart hath daily burned,
But now I rest.

Nature's self seemed clothed in mourning;
Even the starlike woodland flower,
With its leaflets fair, adorning
The pathway to the forest bower,
Drooped its head.

From the cavern of the mountain,
From the groves that crown the hill,
From the stream and from the fountain,
Sounds prophetic murmured still,
Betokening grief.

Boding winds came fitful, sighing,
Through the tall and leafy trees;
Birds of omen, wildly crying,
Sent their calls upon the breeze
Wailing round me.

At each sound I paled and trembled,
At each step I raised my head,
Hearkening if it his resembled,
Or of news that he was dead
Were come from far

All my days were days of weeping;
Thoughts of grim despair were stirred;
Time on leaden feet seemed creeping;
Long heartsickness, hope deferred,
Cankered my heart.

Here the music and singing suddenly ceased. Albion raised
his head. All was darkness except where the silver moonbeams

showed a desolate and ruined apartment, instead of the elegant parlour that a few minutes before had gladdened his sight. No trace of Marina was visible, no harp or other instrument of harmony; and the cold lunar light streamed through a void space instead of the glass door. He sprang up, and called aloud:

'Marina! Marina!' But only an echo as of empty rooms answered. Almost distracted, he rushed into the open air. A child was standing alone at the garden gate, who advanced towards him and said:

'I will lead you to Marina Angus. She has removed from that house to another.'

Albion followed the child till they came to a long row of tall dark trees leading to a churchyard, which they entered, and the child vanished, leaving Albion beside a white marble tombstone on which was chiselled:

MARINA ANGUS
She died
18th of June 1815
at
12 o'clock midnight.

When Albion had read this, he felt a pang of horrible anguish wring his heart and convulse his whole frame. With a loud groan he fell across the tomb and lay there senseless a long time, till at length he was waked from the deathlike trance to behold the spirit of Marina, which stood beside him a moment, and then, murmuring, 'Albion, I am happy, for I am at peace,' disappeared!

For a few days he lingered round her tomb, and then quitted Strathelleraye, where he was never again heard of.

The reason of Marina's death I shall briefly relate. Four years after Albion's departure, tidings came to the village that he was dead. The news broke Marina's faithful heart. The day after, she was no more.

The Rivals

LADY ELLRINGTON: 'Tis eve: how that rich sunlight streameth through
The inwoven arches of this sylvan roof!
How those long, lustrous lines of light illume,
With trembling radiance, all the agèd boles
Of elms majestic as the lofty columns
That proudly rear their tall forms to the dome
Of old cathedral or imperial palace!
Yea, they are grander than the mightiest shafts
That e'er by hand of man were fashioned forth
Their holy, solemn temples to uphold.
And sweeter far than the harmonious peals
Of choral thunder, that in music roll
Through vaulted isles, are the low forest sounds
Murmuring around; of wind and stirrèd leaf,
And warbled song of nightingale or lark,
Whose swelling cadences and dying falls
And whelming gushes of rich melody
Attune to meditation, all serene,
The weary spirit, and draw forth still thoughts
Of happy scenes half veilèd by the mists
Of bygone times. Yea, that calm influence
Hath soothed the billowy troubles of my heart
Till scarce one sad thought rises, though I sit
Beneath these trees, utterly desolate.
But no, not utterly, for still one friend
I fain would hope remains to brighten yet

My mournful journey through this vale of tears;
And, while he shines, all other, lesser lights
May wane and fade unnoticed from the sky.
But more than friend, e'en he can never be.
[*heaves a deep sigh*]
That thought is sorrowful, but yet I'll hope.
What is my rival? Nought but a weak girl,
Ungifted with the state and majesty
That mark superior minds. Her eyes gleam not
Like windows to a soul of loftiness;
She hath not raven locks that lightly wave
Over a brow whose calm placidity
Might emulate the white and polished marble.
[*A white dove flutters by.*]
Ha! What art thou, fair creature? It hath vanished
Down that vista of low-drooping trees.
How gracefully its pinions waved! Methinks
It was the spirit of this solitude.
List! I hear footsteps, and the rustling leaves
Proclaim the approach of some corporeal being.

[*A young girl advances up the vista, dressed in green, with a garland of flowers wreathed in the curls of her hazel hair. She comes towards* LADY ZENOBIA, *and says:*]

Lady, methinks I erst have seen thy face.
Art thou not that Zenobia, she whose name
Renown hath borne e'en to this far retreat?
LADY ELLRINGTON: Aye, maiden, thou hast rightly guessed.
But how
Did'st recognise me?
GIRL: In Verreopolis[22]

I saw thee walking mid those gardens fair
That like a rich, embroidered belt surround
That mighty city, and one bade me look
At her whose genius had illumined bright
Her age, and country, with undying splendour.
The majesty of thy imperial form,
The fire and sweetness of thy radiant eye,
Alike conspired to impress thine image
Upon my memory, and thus it is
That I know thee as thou sittest there
Queen-like, beneath the over-shadowing boughs
Of that huge oak tree, monarch of this wood.

LADY ELLRINGTON [*smiling graciously*]: Who art thou, maiden?

GIRL: Marian is my name.

LADY ELLRINGTON [*starting up, aside*]: Ha! My rival! [*sternly*] What dost thou here alone?

MARIAN [*aside*]: How her tongue changed! [*aloud*] My favourite cushat dove,
Whose plumes are whiter than new-fallen snow,
Hath wandered, heedless, from my vigilant care.
I saw it gleaming through these dusky trees,
Fair as a star, while soft it glided by,
So have I come to find and lure it back.

LADY ELLRINGTON: Are all thy affections centred in a bird?
For thus thou speakest, as though nought were worthy
Of thought or care saving a silly dove!

MARIAN: Nay, lady, I've a father, and mayhap
Others whom gratitude or tenderer ties,
If such there be, bind my heart closely to.

LADY ELLRINGTON: But birds and flowers and such trifles vain

Seem most to attract thy love, if I may form
A judgement from thy locks elaborate curled
And wreathed about with woven garlandry,
And from thy whining speech, all redolent
With tone of most affected sentiment.
[*She seizes* MARIAN, *and exclaims with a violent gesture*]
Wretch, I could kill thee!

MARIAN: Why, what have I done?
How have I wronged thee? Surely thou'rt distraught!

LADY ELLRINGTON: How hast thou wronged me? Where didst weave the net
Whose cunning meshes have entangled round
The mightiest heart that e'er in mortal breast
Did beat responsive unto human feeling?

MARIAN: The net? What net? I wove no net; she's frantic!

LADY ELLRINGTON: Dull, simple creature! Can'st not understand?

MARIAN: Truly, I cannot. 'Tis to me a problem,
An unsolved riddle, an enigma dark.

LADY ELLRINGTON: I'll tell thee, then. But, hark! What voice is that?

VOICE [*from the forest*]: Marian, where art thou? I have found a rose
Fair as thyself. Come hither, and I'll place it
With the blue violets on thine ivory brow.

MARIAN: He calls me; I must go; restrain me not.

LADY ELLRINGTON: Nay, I will hold thee firmly as grim death.
Thou needst not struggle, for my grasp is strong.
Thou shalt not go; Lord Arthur shall come here,
And I will gain the rose despite of thee!
Now for mine hour of triumph. Here he comes.

[LORD ARTHUR *advances from among the trees, exclaims on seeing* LADY ELLRINGTON.]

LORD ARTHUR: Zenobia! How cam'st thou here? What ails
    thee?
    Thy cheek is flushed as with a fever glow;
    Thine eyes flash strangest radiance; and thy frame
    Trembles like to the wind-stirred aspen tree!
LADY ELLRINGTON: Give me the rose, Lord Arthur, for
    methinks
    I merit it more than my girlish rival;
    I pray thee now grant my request, and place
    That rose upon my forehead, not on hers.
    Then I will serve thee all my after-days
    As thy poor handmaid, as thy humblest slave,
    Happy to kiss the dust beneath thy tread,
    To kneel submissive in thy lordly presence.
    Oh! Turn thine eyes from her and look on me
    As I lie here imploring at thy feet,
    Supremely blest if but a single glance
    Could tell me thou art not wholly deaf
    To my petition, earnestly preferred.
LORD ARTHUR: Lady, thou'st surely mad! Depart, and hush
    These importunate cries. They are not worthy
    Of the great name which thou hast fairly earned.
LADY ELLRINGTON: Give me that rose, or I to thee will cleave
    Till death these vigorous sinews has unstrung.
    Hear me this once and give it me Lord Arthur.
LORD ARTHUR [*after a few minutes' deliberation*]: Here, take
    the flower, and keep it for my sake.

[MARIAN *utters a suppressed scream, and sinks to the ground.*]

Lady Ellrington [*assisting her to rise*]: Now I have triumphed! But I'll not exult;
Yet know, henceforth, I'm thy superior.
Farewell, my lord; I thank thee for thy preference!
[*plunges into the wood and disappears*]

Lord Arthur: Fear nothing, Marian, for a fading flower
Is not symbolical of constancy.
But take this sign; [*gives her his diamond ring*] enduring adamant
Betokens well affection that will live
Long as life animates my faithful heart.
Now let us go, for see, the deepening shades
Of twilight darken our lone forest path,
And, lo! thy dove comes gliding through the mirk,
Fair wanderer, back to its loved mistress' care!
Luna[23] will light us on our journey home,
For see, her lamp shines radiant in the sky,
And her bright beams will pierce the thickest boughs.

[*Exeunt, curtain falls.*]

The Bridal

CHAPTER ONE

In the autumn of the year 1881, being weary of study, and the melancholy solitude of the vast streets and mighty commercial marts of our great Babel, and being fatigued with the ever-resounding thunder of the sea, with the din of a thousand self-moving engines, with the dissonant cries of all nations, kindreds and tongues; in one word, being tired of Verdopolis and all its magnificence, I determined on a trip into the country. Accordingly, the day after this resolution was formed, I rose with the sun, collected a few essential articles of dress, packed them neatly in a light knapsack, arranged my apartment, partook of a wholesome repast, and then, after locking the door and delivering the key to my landlady, I set out with a light heart and joyous step.

After three days of continuous travel, I arrived on the banks of a wide and profound river, winding through a vast valley embosomed in hills whose robe of rich and flowery verdure was broken only by the long shadow of groves, and here and there by clustering herds and flocks lying, white as snow, in the green hollows between the mountains. It was the evening of a calm summer day when I reached this enchanting spot. The only sounds now audible were the songs of shepherds, swelling and dying at intervals and the murmur of gliding waves.

I neither knew nor cared where I was. My bodily faculties of eye and ear were absorbed in the contemplation of this delightful scene, and, wandering unheedingly along, I left the guidance of the river and entered a wood, invited by the warbling of a hundred forest minstrels. Soon I perceived the narrow, tangled wood-path to widen, and gradually it assumed the appearance of a green, shady alley.

At length I entered a glade in the wood, in the middle of which was a small but exquisitely beautiful marble edifice of pure and dazzling whiteness. On the broad steps of the portico two figures were reclining, at sight of whom I instantly stepped behind a low, wide-spreading fig tree, where I could hear and see all that passed without fear of detection. One was a youth of lofty stature and remarkably graceful demeanour, attired in a rich purple vest and mantle, with closely fitting white pantaloons of woven silk, displaying to advantage the magnificent proportions of his form. A richly adorned belt was girt tightly round his waist from which depended a scimitar whose golden hilt, and scabbard of the finest Damascus steel, glittered with gems of inestimable value. His steel-barred cap, crested with small, snowy plumes, lay beside him, its absence revealing more clearly the rich curls of dark, glossy hair clustering round a countenance distinguished by the noble beauty of its features, but still more by the radiant fire of genius and intellect visible in the intense brightness of his large, dark and lustrous eyes.

The other form was that of a very young and slender girl, whose complexion was delicately, almost transparently, fair. Her cheeks were tinted with a rich, soft crimson, her features moulded in the utmost perfection of loveliness, while the clear light of her brilliant hazel eyes, and the soft waving of her auburn ringlets, gave additional charms to what seemed already infinitely too beautiful for this earth. Her dress was a white robe of the finest texture the Indian loom can produce. The only ornaments she wore were a long chain which encircled her neck twice and hung lower than her waist, composed of alternate beads of the finest emeralds and gold; and a slight gold ring on the third finger of her left hand, which, together with a small crescent of pearls glistening on her forehead (which is always worn by the noble matrons of Verdopolis), betokened that she had entered the path of wedded life. With a sweet vivacity in her look and manner, the young bride was addressing her lord thus, when I came in sight of the peerless pair:

'No, no, my lord; if I sing the song, you shall choose it. Now, once more, what shall I sing? The moon is risen, and, if your decision is not prompt, I will not sing at all!'

To this he answered, 'Well, if I am threatened with the entire loss of the pleasure if I defer my choice, I will have that sweet song which I overheard you singing before I left Scotland.'

With a smiling blush she took a little ivory lyre, and, in a voice of the most touching melody, sang the following stanzas:

A dark veil is hung
O'er the bright sky of gladness,
And, where birds sweetly sung,
There's a murmur of sadness;
The wind sings with a warning tone
Through many a shadowy tree;
I hear, in every passing moan,
The voice of destiny.

When the lady had concluded her song, I stepped from my place of concealment, and was instantly perceived by the noble youth (whom, of course, every reader will have recognised as the Marquis of Douro). He gave me a courteous welcome, and invited me to proceed with him to his country palace, as it was now wearing late. I willingly accepted the invitation, and, in a short time, we arrived there.

CHAPTER TWO

It is a truly noble structure, built in the purest style of Grecian architecture, situated in the midst of a vast park: embosomed in richly wooded hills, perfumed with orange and citron groves, and watered by a branch of the Gambia, almost equal in size to the parent stream.

The magnificence of the interior is equal to that of the outside. There is an air of regal state and splendour, throughout all the lofty domed apartments, which strikes the spectator with awe for the lord of so imposing a residence. The Marquis has a particular pride in the knowledge that he is the owner of one of the most splendid, select and extensive libraries now in the possession of any individual. His picture and statue galleries likewise contain many of the finest works, both of the ancient and modern masters, particularly the latter, of whom the Marquis is a most generous and munificent patron. In his cabinet of curiosities I observed a beautiful casket of wrought gold. I likewise noticed a brace of pistols, most exquisitely wrought and highly furnished.

[The Marquis' list of treasures, most of which reflect on his own glory, includes 100 gold and silver medals (literary and scientific honours); a gold vase (for composition of the best Greek epigram); a silver bow and quiver (for excellence in archery); a gold bit, bridle and spurs (for horsemanship); several dried wreaths of myrtle and laurel.]

But what interested me more than all these trophies of victory and specimens of art and nature – costly, beautiful and almost invaluable as they were – was a little figure of Apollo, about six inches in height, curiously carved in white agate, holding a lyre in his hand, and placed on a pedestal of the same valuable material, in which was the following inscription:

In our day we beheld the god of Archery, Eloquence and Verse, shrined in an infinitely fairer form than that worn by the ancient Apollo, and giving far more glorious proofs of his divinity than the day god ever vouchsafed to the inhabitants of the old pagan world. Zenobia Ellrington implores Arthur Augustus Wellesley to accept this small memorial, and consider it as a token that, though forsaken and despised by him whose good opinion and friendship she valued more than life, she yet bears no malice.

There was a secret contained in this inscription which I could not fathom. I had never before heard of any misunderstanding between His Lordship and Lady Zenobia, nor did public appearances warrant a suspicion of its existence. Long after, however, the following circumstances came to my knowledge. The channel through which they reached me cannot be doubted, but I am not at liberty to mention names.

CHAPTER THREE

One evening about dusk, as the Marquis of Douro was returning from a shooting excursion into the country, he heard suddenly a rustling noise in a deep ditch on the roadside. He was preparing his fowling piece for a shot when the form of Lady Ellrington started up before him. Her head was bare, her tall person was enveloped in the tattered remnants of a dark velvet mantle. Her dishevelled hair hung in wild elflocks over her face, neck and shoulders, almost concealing her features, which were emaciated and pale as death. He stepped back a few paces, startled at the sudden and ghastly apparition. She threw herself on her knees before him, exclaiming in wild, maniacal accents:

'My lord, tell me truly, sincerely, ingenuously, where you have been. I heard that you had left Verdopolis, and I followed you on foot five hundred miles. Then my strength failed me, and I lay down in this place, as I thought, to die. But it was doomed I should see you once more before I became an inhabitant of the grave. Answer me, my lord: have you seen that wretch Marian Hume? Have you spoken to her? Viper! Viper! Oh, that I could sheathe this weapon in her heart!'

Here she stopped for want of breath, and, drawing a long, sharp, glittering knife from under her cloak, brandished it wildly in the air. The Marquis looked at her steadily, and, without attempting to disarm her, answered with great composure:

'You have asked me a strange question, Lady Zenobia, but before I attempt to answer it, you had better come with me to our encampment. I will order a tent to be prepared for you where you may pass the night in safety, and tomorrow, when you are a little recruited by rest and refreshment, we will discuss this matter soberly.'

Her rage was now exhausted by its own vehemence, and she replied with more calmness than she had hitherto evinced, 'My lord, believe me, I am deputed by Heaven to warn you of a great danger into which you are about to fall. If you persist in your intention of uniting yourself to Marian Hume you will become a murderer and a suicide. I cannot now explain myself more clearly, but ponder carefully on my words until I see you again.'

Then, bowing her forehead to the earth in an attitude of adoration, she kissed his feet, muttering at the same time some unintelligible words. At that moment a loud rushing, like the sound of a whirlwind, became audible, and Lady Zenobia was swept away by some invisible power before the Marquis could extend his arm to arrest her progress, or frame an answer to her mysterious address. He paced slowly forward, lost in deep reflection on what he had heard and seen. The moon had risen over the black, barren mountains ere he reached the camp. He gazed for a while on her pure, undimmed lustre, comparing it to the loveliness of one far away, and then, entering his tent, wrapped himself in his hunter's cloak and lay down to unquiet sleep.

Months rolled away and the mystery remained unsolved. Lady Zenobia Ellrington appeared as usual in that dazzling circle of which she was ever a distinguished ornament. There was no trace of wandering fire in her eyes which might lead a careful observer to imagine that her mind was unsteady. Her voice was more subdued and her looks pale, and it was remarked by some that she avoided all (even the most commonplace) communication with the Marquis.

In the mean time the Duke of Wellington had consented to see his son's union with the beautiful, virtuous and accomplished, but untitled, Marian Hume. Vast and splendid preparations were in the making for the approaching bridal, when just at this critical juncture news arrived of the Great Rebellion headed by Alexander Rogue. The intelligence fell with the suddenness and violence of a thunderbolt. Unequivocal symptoms of dissatisfaction began to appear at the same time among the lower orders in Verdopolis. The workmen at the principal mills and furnaces struck for an advance in wages, and, the masters refusing to comply with their exorbitant demands, they all turned out simultaneously. Shortly after, Colonel Grenville, one of the great mill owners, was shot. His assassins, being quickly discovered and delivered up to justice, were interrogated by torture, but they remained inflexible, not a single satisfactory answer being elicited from them.

The police were now doubled. Bands of soldiers were stationed in the more suspicious parts of the city, and orders were issued that no citizen should walk abroad unarmed. In this state of affairs Parliament was summoned to consult on the best measures to be taken. On the first night of its sitting the house was crowded to excess. All the members attended, and above a thousand ladies of the first rank appeared in the gallery. A settled expression of gloom and anxiety was visible in every countenance. They sat for some time gazing at each other in the silence of seeming despair.

At length the Marquis of Douro rose and ascended the tribunal. It was on this memorable night he pronounced that celebrated oration which will be delivered to farthest posterity as a finished specimen of the sublimest eloquence. The souls of all who heard him were thrilled with conflicting emotions. Some of the ladies in the gallery fainted and were carried out. My limits will not permit me to transcribe the whole of this speech, and to attempt an abridgement would be profanation. I will, however, present the reader with the conclusion. It was as follows:

'I'll call on you, my countrymen, to rouse yourselves to action. There is a latent flame of rebellion smouldering in our city, which blood alone can quench: the hot blood of ourselves and our enemies freely poured forth! We daily see in our streets men whose brows were once open as the day, but which are now wrinkled with dark dissatisfaction, and the light of whose eyes, formerly free as sunshine, is now dimmed by restless suspicion. Our upright merchants are ever threatened with fears of assassination from those dependants who, in time past, loved, honoured and reverenced them as fathers. Our peaceful citizens cannot pass their thresholds in safety unless laden with weapons of war, the continual dread of death haunting their footsteps wherever they turn. And who has produced this awful change? What agency of hell had effected, what master spirit of crime, what prince of sin, what Beelzebub of black iniquity, has been at work in the kingdom? I will answer that fearful question: Alexander Rogue! Arm for the battle, then, fellow-countrymen; be not faint-hearted, but trust in the justice of your cause as your banner of protection, and let your war shout in the onslaught ever be: "God defend the right!"'

When the Marquis had concluded this harangue, he left the house amidst long and loud thunders of applause, and proceeded to a shady grove on the river-banks. Here he walked for some time inhaling the fresh night wind, which acquired additional coolness as it swept over the broad rapid river; he was just beginning to recover from the strong excitement into which his enthusiasm had thrown him, when he felt his arm suddenly grasped from behind, and turning round, beheld Lady Zenobia Ellrington standing beside him, with the same wild, unnatural expression of countenance which had before convulsed her features.

'My lord,' she muttered, in a low, energetic tone, 'your eloquence, your noble genius has again driven me to desperation. I am no longer mistress of myself, and if you do not consent to be mine, and mine alone, I will kill myself where I stand.'

'Lady Ellrington,' said the Marquis coldly, withdrawing his hand from her grasp, 'this conduct is unworthy of your character. I must beg that you will cease to use the language of a madwoman, for I do assure you, my lady, these deep stratagems will have no effect upon me.'

She now threw herself at his feet, exclaiming in a voice almost stifled with ungovernable emotion, 'Oh! do not kill me with such cold, cruel disdain. Only consent to follow me, and you will be convinced that you ought not to be united to one so utterly unworthy of you as Marian Hume.'

The Marquis, moved by her tears and entreaties, at length consented to accompany her. She led him a considerable distance from the city to a subterraneous grotto, where was a fire burning on a brazen altar. She threw a certain powder into the flame, and immediately they were transported through the air to an apartment at the summit of a lofty tower. At one end of this room was a vast mirror, and at the other a drawn curtain, behind which a most brilliant light was visible.

'You are now,' said Lady Ellrington, 'in the sacred presence of one whose counsel, I am sure, you, my lord, will never slight.'

At this moment the curtain was removed, and the astonished Marquis beheld Crashie,[24] the divine and infallible, seated on his golden throne, and surrounded by those mysterious rays of light which ever emanate from him.

'My son,' said he, with an august smile, and in a voice of awful harmony, 'fate and inexorable destiny have decreed that in the hour you are united to the maiden of your choice, the angel Azazel[25] shall smite you both, and convey your disembodied souls over the swift-flowing and impassable river of death. Hearken to the counsels of wisdom, and do not, in the madness of self-will, destroy yourself and Marian Hume by

108

refusing the offered hand of one who, from the moment of your birth, was doomed by the prophetic stars of heaven to be your partner and support through the dark, unexplored wilderness of future life.'

He ceased. The combat betwixt true love and duty raged for a few seconds in the Marquis' heart, and sent his lifeblood in a tumult of agony and despair burning to his cheek and brow. At length duty prevailed, and, with a strong effort, he said in a firm, unfaltering voice:

'Son of Wisdom! I will war no longer against the high decree of Heaven, and here I swear by the eternal '

The rash oath was checked in the moment of its utterance by some friendly spirit who whispered in his ear, 'This is magic. Beware.'

At the same instant Crashie's venerable form faded away, and in its stead appeared the evil genius, Danhasch,[26] in all the naked hideousness of his real deformity. The demon soon vanished with a wild howl of rage, and the Marquis found himself again in the grove with Lady Ellrington.

She implored him on her knees to forgive an attempt which love alone had dictated, but he turned from her with a smile of bitter contempt and disdain, and hastened to his father's palace.

About a week after this event the nuptials of Arthur Augustus, Marquis of Douro, and Marian Hume were solemnised with unprecedented pomp and splendour. Lady Ellrington, when she thus saw that all her hopes were lost in despair, fell into deep melancholy, and while in this state she amused herself with carving the little image before-mentioned. After a long time she slowly recovered, and the Marquis, convinced that her extravagances had arisen from a disordered brain, consented to honour her with his friendship once more.

I continued upwards of two months at the Marquis of Douro's country place, and then returned to Verdopolis, equally delighted with my noble host and his fair, amiable bride.

A Peep into a Picture Book

It is a fine, warm, sultry day, just after dinner. I am at Thornton Hotel. The General is enjoying his customary nap; and while the serene evening sunshine reposes on his bland features and unruffled brow, an atmosphere of calm seems to pervade the apartment.

What shall I do to amuse myself? I dare not stir lest he should awake, and any disturbance of his slumbers at this moment might be productive of serious consequences to me: no circumstance would more effectively sour my landlord's ordinarily bland temperament. Hark! there is a slight, light snore, most musical, most melancholy; he is firmly locked in the chains of the drowsy god. I will try. At the opposite end of the room three large volumes that look like picture books lie on a sideboard; their green watered-silk quarto covers and gilt backs are tempting, and I will make an effort to gain possession of them.

With zephyr-step and bosomed breath I glide onward to the sideboard; I seize my prize; catlike I creep back and being once more established in my chair I open the volumes to see if the profit be equivalent to the pains.

A mighty phantom has answered my spell; an awful shape clouds the magic mirror! Reader, before me I behold the earthly tabernacle of Northangerland's unsounded soul![27] There he stands, what a vessel to be moulded from the coarse clay of mortality! What a plant to spring from the rank soil of human existence! And the vessel is without flaw: polished, fresh and bright from the last process of the maker. The flower has sprung up to mature beauty, but not a leaf is curled, not a blossom faded. This portrait was taken ere the lights and shadows of twenty-five summers had fallen across the wondrous labyrinth of Percy's path through life. Percy! Percy! Never was humanity fashioned in a fairer mould. The eye

113

follows, delighted, all those classic lines of face and form; not one unseemly curvature or angle to disturb the general effect of so much refined regularity; all appears carved in ivory. The grossness of flesh and blood will not suit its statuesque exactness and speckless polish. A feeling of fascination comes over me while I gaze on that Phidian[28] nose, defined with such beautiful precision; that chin and mouth chiselled to such elaborate perfection; that high, pale forehead, not bald as now, but yet not shadowed with curls, for the clustering hair is parted back, gathered in abundant wreaths on the temples, and leaving the brow free for all the gloom and glory of a mind that has no parallel to play over the expanse of living marble which its absence reveals. The expression in this picture is somewhat pensive, composed, free from sarcasm except the fixed sneer of the lip and the strange deadly glitter of the eye whose glance – a mixture of the keenest scorn and deepest thought – curdles the spectator's blood to ice. In my opinion this head embodies the most vivid ideas we can conceive of Lucifer, the rebellious archangel: there is such a total absence of human feeling and sympathy; such a cold frozen pride; such a fathomless power of intellect; such passionless yet perfect beauty – not breathing and burning and full of lightning, blood and fiery thought and feeling like that of some others whom our readers will recollect – but severely studied, faultlessly refined, as cold and hard and polished and perfect as the most priceless brilliant. Northangerland has a black drop in his veins that flows through every vessel, taints every limb, stagnates round his heart, and there, in the very citadel of life, turns the glorious blood of the Percys to the bitterest, rankest gall. Let us leave him in that shape, bright with beauty, dark with crime. Farewell, Percy!

I turn the leaves and behold – his countess![29] What eyes! What raven hair! What an imposing contour of form and countenance! She is perfectly grand in her velvet robes, dark plume and crown-like turban. The lady of Ellrington House, the wife of Northangerland, the prima donna of the Angrian court, the most learned woman of her age, the modern Cleopatra, the Verdopolitan de Staël: in a word Zenobia Percy! Who would think that that grand form of feminine majesty could launch out into the unbridled excesses of passion in which Her Ladyship not infrequently indulges? There is fire in her eyes and command on her brow, and some touch of pride that would spurn restraint in the curl of her rich lip. But all is so tempered with womanly dignity that it would seem as if neither fire nor pride nor imperiousness could awaken the towering fits of ungoverned and frantic rage that often deform her beauty.

I have watched him[30] for hours while he sat on a sofa with his lovely wife beside him, and the youthful Marchioness of Douro[31] sitting at his feet, and heard the benignant simplicity with which he poured out the stories of his varied and extensive erudition, answering so kindly and familiarly each question of the fair listeners, mingling an air of conjugal tenderness in his manner to his wife, and an earnest melancholy gentleness in that to Marian such as always characterised his treatment of her. Poor thing! She looked on him as her only friend: her brother, her adviser, her unerring oracle. With the warm devotedness that marked her disposition, she followed his advice as if it had been the precept of inspired revelation. Fidena could not err; he could neither think nor act wrongly; he was perfect. Those who thought him proud were very much mistaken. *She* had never found him so. Nobody had milder and softer manners; nobody spoke more pleasingly. Thus she would talk and then blush with anger if anyone contradicted her too exclusively favourable opinion. Fidena, I believe, regarded Marian as a delicate flower planted in a stormy situation, as a lovely, fragile being that needed his careful protection; and that protection he would have extended to her at the hazard of life itself. To the last he tried to support her. Many lone days he spent in watching and cheering her during her final lingering sickness. But for all the kindness, all the tenderness in the world were insufficient to raise that blighted lily, so long as the sunshine of those eyes which had been her idolatry was withered, and so long as the music of that voice she had loved so fondly and truly sounded too far off to be heard.

Fidena was in the house when she died. On quitting the bedside, as he hung over his adopted sister for the last time, a single large tear dropped on the little worn hand he held in his, and he muttered half aloud:

'Would to god I had possessed this treasure; it should not thus have been thrown away.'

Marian's portrait comes next to Fidena. Everyone knows what it is like: the small delicate features, dark blue eyes full of warm and tender enthusiasm, beautiful nutty curls and frail-looking form, are familiar to all, so I need not pause on a more elaborate detail.

Fire! Light! What have we here? Zamorna's self,[32] blazing in the frontispiece like the sun on his own standard. All his usual insufferableness or irresistibleness, or whatever the ladies choose to call it, surrounding him like an atmosphere, he stands as if a thunderbolt could neither blast the light of his eyes nor dash the effrontery of his brow. Keen, glorious being! Tempered and bright and sharp and rapid as the scimitar at his side, when whirled by the delicate yet vigorous hand that now grasps the bridle of a horse, to all appearance as viciously beautiful as himself. Oh Zamorna! What eyes those are glancing under the deep shadow of that raven crest! They bode no good. Man nor woman could ever gather more than a troubled, fitful happiness from their kindest light. Satan gave them their glory to deepen the midnight gloom that always follows where their lustre has fallen most lovingly. This, indeed, is something different from Percy. All here is passion and fire unquenchable. Impetuous sin, stormy pride, diving and soaring enthusiasm, war and poetry, are kindling their fires in all his veins, and his wild blood boils from his heart and back again like a torrent of new-sprung lava. Young duke? Young demon! I have looked at you till words seemed to issue from your lips in those fine electric tones, as clear and profound as the silver chords of a harp, which steals affections like a charm. I think I see him bending his head to speak to some lady while he whispers words that touch the heart like a melody that's sweetly playing in tune. A low wind rises, sighs slowly onward. Suddenly his plumes rustle; their haughty shadow sweeps over his forehead; the eye – the full, dark, refulgent eye – lightens most gloriously; his curls are all stirred; smiles dawn on his lips. Suddenly he lifts his head, flings back the feathers and clusters of bright hair. And, while he stands erect and godlike, his *regards* (as the French say) bent on the lady, whoever it be – who by this time is, of course, seriously debating whether he be man or angel – a momentary play of indescribable expression round the mouth, and a faint elevation of the eyebrows, tell how the stream of thought runs at that moment; the mind which so noble a form enshrines! Detestable wretch! I hate him!

But just opposite, separated only by a transparent sheet of silver paper, there is something different: his wife, his own matchless Henrietta! She looks at him with her serene eyes as if the dew of placid thought could be shed on his heart by the influence of those large, clear stars. It reminds me of moonlight descending on troubled waters. I wish the parallel held good all the way, and that she was as far beyond the reach of sorrows arising from her husband's insatiable ambition and fiery impetuosity as Diana is above the lash of the relentless deep.[33] But it is not so; her destiny is linked with his. And however strangely the great river of Zamorna's fate may flow, however awful the rapids over which it may rush, however cold and barren the banks of its channel and however wild, however darkly beached and stormily billowed the ocean into which it may finally plunge, Mary's must follow. Fair creature! I could weep to think of it. For her sake, I hope a bright futurity lies before her lord. Pity that the shadow of grief should ever fall where the light of such beauty shines. Everyone knows how like the Duchess is to her father;[34] his very image cast in a softer – it could not be a more refined – mould. As Byron says, her features have all the statuesque repose, the calm classic grace, that dwell on the Earl's. She, however, has one advantage over him: the stealing, pensive brilliance of her hazel eyes, and the peaceful sweetness of her mouth, impart a harmony to the whole which the satanic sneer fixed on the corresponding features of Northangerland's face totally destroys.

NOTES

1. Verdopolis is Greek for 'Glass Town', the name the Brontës adopted for the setting of much of their juvenilia.

2. In her juvenilia, Charlotte Brontë frequently wrote in the character of Charles Wellesley, her brother being Arthur Wellesley, Marquis of Douro, and their father the Duke of Wellington.

3. 'former dear friend' (French).

4. Here a name is missing due to an indecipherable section of the manuscript.

5. The lines are adapted from *The Traveller*, by Oliver Goldsmith (ll. 327–8):
'Pride in their port, defiance in their eye,/ I see the lords of humankind pass by'.

6. 'holy of holies' (Latin.) The original reference is to the inner sanctuary of the tabernacle, which contained the ark of the covenant (Exodus 25: 10–16).

7. In the Brontës' juvenilia Alexander the First was the monarchical title of Alexander Sneaky, King of Sneachieland. In 'Lily Hart', he is referred to as 'Monarch of the mountains'.

8. The four Great Genii – Tali, Brani, Emi, and Anni – were Charlotte, Branwell, Emily and Anne Brontë respectively.

9. General Bobadil also features in Brontë's *The Green Dwarf*. Captain Bobadil was originally the name of a character in Ben Jonson's *Every Man in his Humour* (1598). The name has come to denote a military braggart.

10. The Great Insurrection is part of the civil war described in Branwell Brontë's 'Letters from an Englishman'. In this narrative, it began on 16 March 1831.

11. The Twelve were the original twelve soldiers who formed the Glasstown Confederacy in the Brontës' juvenilia. Here it stands for 'one of the Twelve'.

12. Albion and Marina are pseudonyms for Brontë's hero Arthur, Marquis of Douro, and his young lover, Marian Hume, who are depicted in 'The Secret' at a later stage of their relationship.

13. 'no sheepshank', i.e. a person of importance (Scots dialect).

14. The pseudonym of Brontë's character the Duke of Wellington.

15. Charles Wellesley, the character usually assumed by Brontë in the position of narrator.

16. i.e. the wing of a hooded crow.

17. The Apollo Belvedere is a renowned marble statue of Apollo, based on a fifth-century BC Greek original, and is currently held in the Vatican.

18. Ninus was a king of Assyria, whose capital was Nineveh, and Belus was the founder of Babylon. Astarte was a Phoenician goddess worshipped in the region of the Mediterranean and North Africa; Semele was the mother of the Greek god Dionysus.

19. Here some text is missing.

20. Lady Zenobia Ellrington.

21. Madame de Staël (1766–1817) was a French novelist and prominent society figure.

22. Glass Town.

23. Luna is the Roman personification of the moon.

24. Crashie is a deity who appears frequently in the Brontës' juvenilia.

25. Azazel is a name given to a number of figures in the Bible, including a goat demon (Leviticus 16–17) and a fallen angel (1 Enoch 8). In Milton's *Paradise Lost* (1667), Azazel is Satan's standard-bearer.

26. Danhasch was the name of an evil genie featured in the *Arabian Nights*.

27. Northangerland was the earldom of Alexander Rogue, the mortal enemy of Arthur, Marquis of Douro.

28. Phidias (490–430 BC) is widely regarded as the finest sculptor of ancient Greece.

29. The Earl of Northangerland's wife was Lady Zenobia Ellrington.

30. This section depicts Prince John of Fidena, the hero of 'Lily Hart'. Some text is missing at the beginning of this passage.

31. Brontë here intends Douro's first wife, Marian.

32. Zamorna is a later dukedom of the Marquis of Douro.

33. Diana was the Roman goddess of hunting, counterpart of the Greek goddess Artemis. Brontë here perhaps refers to her untouchable virginity.

34. Douro's second wife, Mary, is Northangerland's daughter.

NOTE ON THE TEXT

The first two stories in this volume, 'The Secret' and 'Lily Hart', were contained in a manuscript of 1833, which was first published in 1908, and subsequently considered lost until rediscovered and transcribed for the first time in 1978. The stories formed part of Charlotte Brontë's cycle of juvenilia concerning the nobility of the kingdom of Angria in Africa. This edition contains a reworked transcription of these two stories, together with four others, 'Albion and Marina' and 'The Rivals', both written in 1830, 'The Bridal', from 1832, and 'A Peep into a Picture Book', written in 1834. These additional stories give a further glimpse into the life and fortunes of the same characters featured in 'The Secret' and 'Lily Hart', and follow Brontë's familiar themes of secrecy, deception and the supernatural. Although Brontë occasionally takes surprising liberties in continuity – even resurrecting the character of Marian, between 'Albion and Marina' and 'The Rivals' – when presented in a single volume, the stories show the breadth of her literary invention and her growing facility with the forms of prose narrative, drama, verse and character sketch.

Charlotte Brontë was born in Thornton, Yorkshire, in 1816. In 1820 her father was appointed curate at Haworth Parsonage where Charlotte was to spend most of her life. Following the death of her mother in 1821 and of her two eldest sisters in 1825, she and her two surviving sisters, Emily and Anne, and brother, Branwell, were brought up by their father and a devoutly religious aunt.

Theirs was an unhappy childhood, in particular the period the sisters spent at a school for daughters of the clergy. Charlotte abhorred the harsh regime, blaming it for the deaths of her two sisters, and she went on to fictionalise her experiences there in *Jane Eyre* (1847). Having been removed from the school, the three sisters, together with Branwell, found solace in storytelling. Inspired by a set of toy soldiers, they created the imaginary kingdoms of Angria and Gondal which form the settings for much of their juvenilia. From 1831 to 1832 Charlotte was educated at Roe Head school where she later returned as a teacher.

In 1842 Charlotte travelled to Brussels with Emily. They returned home briefly following the death of their aunt, but, soon after, Charlotte was back in Brussels, this time as a teacher. At great expense the three sisters published a volume of poetry – *Poems by Currer, Ellis and Acton Bell* (1846) – but this proved unsuccessful, selling only two copies. By the time of its publication, each of the sisters had completed a novel: Emily's *Wuthering Heights* and Anne's *Agnes Grey* were both published in 1847, but Charlotte's novel, *The Professor*, remained unpublished in her lifetime. Undeterred, Charlotte embarked on *Jane Eyre*, which was also published in 1847 and hailed by Thackeray as 'the masterwork of a great genius'. She followed this up with *Shirley* (1849) and *Villette* (1853), and continued to be published under the pseudonym Currer Bell although her identity was, by now, well known.

Branwell, in many ways the least successful of the four siblings, died in 1848. His death deeply distressed the sisters, and both Emily and Anne died within the following year. Charlotte married her father's curate in 1854, but she died in the early stages of pregnancy in March 1855.

HESPERUS PRESS CLASSICS

Hesperus Press, as suggested by the Latin motto, is committed to bringing near what is far – far both in space and time. Works written by the greatest authors, and unjustly neglected or simply little known in the English-speaking world, are made accessible through new translations and a completely fresh editorial approach. Through these classic works, the reader is introduced to the greatest writers from all times and all cultures.

For more information on Hesperus Press, please visit our website: **www.hesperuspress.com**

ET REMOTISSIMA PROPE

SELECTED TITLES FROM HESPERUS PRESS

Author	Title	Foreword writer
Jane Austen	*Love and Friendship*	Fay Weldon
Aphra Behn	*The Lover's Watch*	
Charlotte Brontë	*The Green Dwarf*	Libby Purves
Emily Brontë	*Poems of Solitude*	Helen Dunmore
Anton Chekhov	*Three Years*	William Fiennes
Wilkie Collins	*Who Killed Zebedee?*	Martin Jarvis
William Congreve	*Incognita*	Peter Ackroyd
Joseph Conrad	*The Return*	Colm Tóibín
Charles Dickens	*The Haunted House*	Peter Ackroyd
Fyodor Dostoevsky	*The Double*	Jeremy Dyson
George Eliot	*Amos Barton*	Matthew Sweet
Henry Fielding	*Jonathan Wild the Great*	Peter Ackroyd
F. Scott Fitzgerald	*The Rich Boy*	John Updike
E.M. Forster	*Arctic Summer*	Anita Desai
Elizabeth Gaskell	*Lois the Witch*	Jenny Uglow
Thomas Hardy	*Fellow-Townsmen*	Emma Tennant
L.P. Hartley	*Simonetta Perkins*	Margaret Drabble
Nathaniel Hawthorne	*Rappaccini's Daughter*	Simon Schama
John Keats	*Fugitive Poems*	Andrew Motion
D.H. Lawrence	*Daughters of the Vicar*	Anita Desai
Katherine Mansfield	*In a German Pension*	Linda Grant
Prosper Mérimée	*Carmen*	Philip Pullman
Sándor Petőfi	*John the Valiant*	George Szirtes
Alexander Pope	*The Rape of the Lock*	Peter Ackroyd
Robert Louis Stevenson	*Dr Jekyll and Mr Hyde*	Helen Dunmore
Leo Tolstoy	*Hadji Murat*	Colm Tóibín
Mark Twain	*Tom Sawyer, Detective*	
Oscar Wilde	*The Portrait of Mr W.H.*	Peter Ackroyd
Virginia Woolf	*Carlyle's House and Other Sketches*	Doris Lessing